W9-BZE-611

CASTLE IN THE AIR

Donald E. Westlake

CASTLE IN THE AIR

M. EVANS AND COMPANY, INC.
New York

UNIVERSITY OF TOLEDO LIBRARIES

Library of Congress Cataloging in Publication Data

Westlake, Donald E
    Castle in the air.

    I. Title.
PZ4.W53Cas [PS3573.E9] 813'.54 79-27514
ISBN 0-87131-322-7

Copyright © 1980 by Donald E. Westlake

All rights reserved. No part of this book may be reproduced
or transmitted in any form or by any means without the written
permission of the publisher.

M. Evans and Company, Inc.
216 East 49 Street
New York, New York 10017

Design by Diane Gedymin

Manufactured in the United States of America

9 8 7 6 5 4 3 2 1

PZ
4
.W53 Cas

And this one is for the guys and gals
at the Internal Revenue Service.

1

Eustace Dench, master criminal, paid the cabby with a legitimate five pound note, accepted his change, gave the man a twenty pence tip—not enough; the chap did *not* touch his cap—and turned away to take the delectable Lida's slender arm. It was not raining, but otherwise it was unmistakably London—Belgravia, Herbert Way, a curving street of magnificent ivory-colored houses, several of them still private residences, the others all converted into embassies, offices, clubs or oil-sheiks' pieds-à-terre. Number nine, with a large black "9" painted on the pillars flanking the entrance, was Eustace's destination: the Tobacco and Artillery Club, founded 1711. "Come along, my dear," he said to the lovely Lida, and they crossed the flagstones.

Inside, Eustace asked for Sir Mortimer Maxwell, identified himself as "Eustace Digby," and was shown up the broad staircase—mahogany and maroon carpeting everywhere—to the members' dining room, where Sir Mortimer was seated by himself at a table, crumbling rolls onto the snowy linen napery and sipping at a glass of gin-and-it, an abysmal cousin of the martini, *reeking* of vermouth. Sir

Mortimer, a stocky broad-shouldered well-dressed man with white hair and moustache, red cheeks and nose, had the look of a former military man and present sot, and his eyes were appropriately bleary when he lifted them to say, "Ah, Eustace."

"Sir Mortimer." The men shook hands, and Eustace said, "May I present Miss Lida Perez, Sir Mortimer Maxwell."

Lida curtsied, as she'd been taught in the convent. Most of the men in the room were looking at her by now, except for those who were looking at the perky new busboy.

"D'je do," Sir Mortimer said. He was too weary for sex.

Eustace and Lida sat at the table, Eustace turned to the waiter to order gin-and-water for himself and rum-and-Coca-Cola for Lida, and then he turned back to explain to Sir Mortimer. "Lida is Yerbadoroan."

Sir Mortimer managed to look sympathetic.

Forcefully, rather more loudly than the setting suggested, Lida said, "My people are oppressed!" Her eyes flashed, her coal-black hair flashed, her teeth flashed. She was the true Latin beauty, fire and ice.

Sir Mortimer looked at her in exhausted surprise. "I beg your pardon?"

"My *people* are *oppressed!*"

"Ah." His expression wistful, Sir Mortimer nodded, saying, "If only I could say the same for mine." To Eustace he said, "On the phone, you suggested you had something useful for me."

"Oh, you'll like this," Eustace said, smiling cheerfully and rubbing his hands together.

"I certainly hope so."

They paused while the waiter delivered their drinks, and then Sir Mortimer went on: "To be frank, old man, I'm on my uppers. You'll see what I mean when the food

8

arrives. Worst sole in London, but this's the last place'll take my signature."

"This little caper's going to change *all* our luck," Eustace assured him.

"Tell me at once."

"The story begins in Yerbadoro," Eustace said. "Lida's brave little nation," he added, patting the girl's forearm.

Lida, fortunately, was drinking rum-and-Coca-Cola at the time, and so couldn't speak. She contented herself with a quick flash of the eyes.

"The president of Yerbadoro," Eustace went on, "is a chap named Lynch. Escobar Lynch."

Sir Mortimer reared back: "You're having me on."

Placing her glass on the table, Lida explained, "In the early nineteenth century, Irish pirates liberated my country from the Spanish."

"Ah hah," said Sir Mortimer.

"This fellow Lynch," Eustace went on, "the president, he's in trouble. Days are numbered. Army coup from the right, urban guerrillas on the left."

"Viva Yerbadoro!" Lida announced, raising a clenched fist.

Eustace patted her arm again, to soothe her. "Yes, yes, Lida, that's right." To Sir Mortimer, he went on, "Lynch wants to get out of the country."

"Can't say I blame him."

"But he can't get his money out, you see."

"Ill-gotten gains," Lida announced, while gentlemen at neighboring tables hunched over their hock. "Blood from the veins of the peasants!"

Sir Mortimer's head shook at the phrase.

"They're watching Lynch too closely," Eustace went on, ignoring Lida's outburst with the readiness of long practice. "Not the guerrillas. The Army, and the right wing.

9

As far as they're concerned, *he* can leave, but not his profits. If he tries to open a Swiss bank account, or travel with all his wife's jewelry—" Eustace slid a graphically illustrative finger across his neck.

Sir Mortimer winced. "Sounds a difficult position."

Leaning closer, lowering his voice, Eustace said, "But he's found a way out."

"Good for him!" Then Sir Mortimer frowned, somewhat baffled. "An Irishman, you say?"

"A Yerbodoroan," Eustace corrected. "A *rich* Yerbadoroan."

"Oh, I *see*. And these ill-gotten gains of his—"

"Exactly." Broadly beaming, Eustace whispered, "Soon they shall be ill-gotten gains of *ours*."

"Tell me more."

"I intend to. You know this exposition coming up soon in Paris?"

Sir Mortimer looked disapproving. "They're always exposing something in Paris," he said.

✽

"Every country involved in the exposition is building a pavilion," Eustace explained, and popped a delicious shrimp into his mouth. "All over the city," he said, and waved an arm to indicate Paris, teeming just beyond the restaurant windows. He was here with Lida, ingesting magnificent bouillabaisse in this tiny Left-Bank restaurant on the Quai des Grands-Augustins, in order to tell his story to Jean LeFraque, a charming debonair middle-aged conman with a sinfully tiny moustache. "Each nation's building," he went on, "will reflect the style and thinking of that nation."

Jean paused briefly in his admiring perusal of Lida to sigh, shake his head, and say, "How I despise architecture."

Peeling the sweet meat from the carapace of a lobster fragment, Eustace said, "Lynch is having a building in Yerbadoro dismantled and shipped here to Paris. A small castle."

Jean permitted himself to look startled. "*Importing* a building to Paris? From South America?"

"Just as London Bridge was transported to Arizona. Just as other buildings and monuments have been moved from place to place."

"The man's mad," Jean decided, and shrugged.

"No, he isn't," Eustace said, and paused to savor his lobster. *So much* better than the Tobacco and Artillery Club sole. "What Lynch has done," he went on, "he's hollowed out a dozen stones, large building blocks from the outer walls of this castle, and he's filled the hollow spaces with cash, jewels, stocks, his entire fortune. Then he's disguised the openings so the stones look exactly as before. But *inside* them are valuables worth millions!"

"The rape of my people!" Lida announced, brandishing her bouillabaisse spoon.

Jean considered her thoughtfully. "Mm, yes," he said.

"Lida's cousin," Eustace went on, "was one of the stonemasons on the project. He was sworn to secrecy, of course, but he told Lida the whole story."

"Before he disappeared," Lida said grimly.

"There's millions in it, Jean," Eustace said.

"Mmmm," Jean said. Behind his dark eyes his brain could be seen ticking away faster than a taxicab meter in Milan. "One sees the possibilities," he acknowledged.

Lida, her expression and posture valiant, clutched Jean's forearm to say, "*You* shall save my people from destitution!"

Jean looked at her askance. "What's this?"

11

"Half," Eustace said. "That's the arrangement I have with Lida."

"What arrangement?" Storm clouds were crossing Jean's face now, and his moustache was at half mast.

"We take half the profit for our work and expenses," Eustace explained, "and the other half goes back to Yerbadoro with Lida." But simultaneously, behind Lida's back, Eustace was briskly waving his hand back and forth, to let Jean know he was lying.

"Ah," Jean said, with a large nod and a small smile, "I see. Well, that sounds fair." To Lida, pouring on the charm, he said, "You are a stirring spokeswoman for your people."

Her response was violent: "I am a fiery furnace for my people!"

Taken aback, Jean retreated into his chair a few inches. "Yes," he said. "Yes, I can see that."

"Now," Eustace said. "The only problem is—"

❖

"Of *course* there's a problem," Rosa Palermo said. Stuffing scungilli and spaghetti into her mouth, she went on talking just the same: "There's *always* a problem, Eustace."

"A small problem, Rosa," Eustace said, with a casual shrug of the shoulders and an airy gesture with his fingers. There was something about lunch at an outdoor restaurant on Rome's Via Veneto that made him more than usually expressive with his body and his hands. "A minor problem," he said. "Nothing that need stop us."

Rosa, a hefty beauty in her mid-forties, aggressive and excitable, swigged down a mouthful of Bardolino and said, "Tell me about this problem, this *minor* problem."

"It's nothing at all," Eustace assured her. He was aware of the male passersby frowning at him, wondering by what system of punishments and rewards a fellow like Eustace Dench deserved to be at table with such a fiery pair of beautiful women; so different from one another but both so desirable. "It's merely," he said, "that we don't know exactly *which* stones we want."

In sudden anger, Rosa flung her fork onto the table, sat back in her chair, squared her shoulders, aimed her breasts at Eustace, and said, "*What?* Then it's useless, we can't do a thing!"

"Of *course* we can—"

"You take me away from a perfectly fine shoplifting operation, you—"

"Rosa, Rosa, wait. It's simple, really, I promise you it is."

"You promise me, do you?" Glaring mistrustfully, Rosa picked up her fork, stuck it into the spaghetti, bore down, and twisted. "Tell me about it," she said.

"We steal the entire castle."

"Steal—?" Rosa's fork halted. She stared at Eustace's smiling confident face, and slowly shook her head. "This girl," she said, with a quick glance at Lida, "has scrambled your brains."

"It can be done, Rosa," Eustace assured her. "You know me, you know my history, I only organize capers of the highest character."

Dubious, Rosa filled her mouth with spaghetti, and chewed. "A whole castle," she said.

"We need more help," Eustace told her. "That's the only thing."

"Oh, yes," Rosa said. "Oh, surely."

"Think of it," Eustace said, leaning toward her, unmindful of his tie in the tomato sauce, "think of it. The best criminal brains in Europe, the *masters,* and each bringing in his own assistants."

Still dubious, Rosa pondered the idea, saying, "Who, for instance?"

"Well, you and me, of course. And from Germany, Herman Muller."

With a judicious nod, Rosa said, "Yes. Yes. I've heard of him."

Eustace checked the names off on his fingers. "From England," he said, "Sir Mortimer Maxwell."

*

"Sir Mortimer," Herman Muller said. "Yes, I worked with him once, in a counterfeiting scheme."

"A good man," Eustace said.

Herman, a skelton-thin smooth and eerie man with a long pockmarked face, shrugged: "A trifie unsocial," he suggested.

"None of us is perfect," Eustace said, and peeled a slice from the large white radish on the side dish. Chewing it, swallowing it with a mouthful of beer, he returned his attention to his bratwurst. Here in the sunny tree-filled central courtyard of Munich's Hofbräuhaus, he and Lida were lunching with their German connection.

Who now said, "Who else?"

"From France," Eustace said, around a pillow of bratwurst, "Jean LeFraque."

Herman considered. "I don't think I know the name."

"A very good man," Eustace assured him. "He's been working American widows recently, in a sort of semi-retirement, but he's been responsible for some of the finest outrages in the files of the Sûreté."

"Widows can ruin a man for serious work," Herman said sternly. "Particularly American widows."

"You don't have to worry about Jean."

Dispassionate, Herman said, "If you say so. Anyone else?"

"From Italy, Rosa Palermo."

Herman stopped with his beer stein halfway to his mouth. For the first time, a bit of color came into his cheeks. He said, "*That* madwoman?"

"Ah," Eustace said, with his blandest smile. "You've heard of her."

"Heard *of* her? On a clear night, you can hear *her*, the other side of the Alps."

"She's a bit excitable," Eustace admitted, "but she's the best."

Herman considered that, frowning. "The best? In Italy, you mean."

"Of course."

"That's possible, I suppose," Herman said, and drank his beer.

"Then you'll head the German contingent," Eustace told him, "and I will serve as liaison among the groups."

❖

"Well, that's the situation," Eustace said, smiling around at his guests. Here in the garden of his little château outside Zurich, with the high privet hedge to guarantee privacy, Eustace and Sir Mortimer Maxwell and Jean LeFraque and Herman Muller and Rosa Palermo and Lida Perez were seated around the white-painted iron lawn table, eating potato pancakes and drinking chablis. The sun shone down, the grass was a rich dark green, the mountains were comfortably massive above the privet hedge, the wine was good, the potato pancakes were as light as clouds, and Eustace basked in a glow of well-being. Not one of his first-choice assistants had turned him down, and he knew full well it wasn't because the caper itself seemed such a sure thing, but because of *him*, his unarguable skill, his enviable reputation. Only Eustace Dench could pull off a heist of such magnitude! To steal an entire castle! Smiling, beaming, already feeling the warmth of the victory to come, he said, "Any questions?"

Sir Mortimer immediately asked the obvious one: "How much is this thing worth?"

"Impossible to say, precisely," Eustace told him. "Best estimates, going on the basis of newspaper accounts of Lynch's probable worth, place our haul at somewhere between ten and twenty-five million pounds."

Sir Mortimer was honestly awed. "Good God," he said.

Rosa Palermo said, "What's that in lire?"

Herman Muller's lip curled. "Seven wheelbarrows full," he said.

"Lire?" Eustace did some fast mental math. "Between sixteen and forty billion."

Rosa merely gaped. *"Billion?"*

"As I said," said Herman.

Jean LeFraque said, "Would you put that in a currency *I* understand?"

"In francs?" Eustace's brain ticked over again. "It would be, in new francs—"

"No, not francs," Jean LeFraque said. "I understand dollars best. U.S."

"In U.S. currency," Eustace told him, "it would be between twenty and fifty million dollars."

"All right," Jean said, smiling, touching his tiny moustache with his fingertips. "Very nice."

Herman said, "What's the split?"

Eustace, with a meaningful look around the table, said, "Well, you know the arrangement with the little lady."

They all looked at Lida, who responded with an expression that was at once embarrassed and determined and valiant. She looked like a figure on a piece of paper money, but without the shield.

"Yes," Jean murmured, "we know about that . . . arrangement."

"So," Eustace said carefully, "we're talking about the remaining *half*."

"Of course," said Herman.

"Well," Eustace said. "I'm taking ten per cent. From the top. Because I'm the one who organized it all in the first place, and I'm to be liaison."

"Yes yes," Rosa said impatiently. "What about the rest?"

"Of the remainder," Eustace said, "there'll be one fifth for each of you. Out of that, you will pay whatever you think appropriate to as many assistants as you think you will require."

Jean said, "Excuse me, Eustace. Permit me to ask more questions, numbers confuse me so. We are talking about in my case twenty per cent of ninety per cent."

With another meaningful look in Lida's direction, Eustace amended, "Of *fifty* per cent."

"Yes, of course," Jean said. "I do apologize. Twenty per cent of ninety per cent of fifty per cent."

"A woman can't deal with things like that," Rosa said briskly. "Just tell me one thing. Will I make a profit?"

"God, yes," Eustace said.

Herman said, "Another question. How do we make the split afterwards?"

"Part of Jean's job," Eustace told him, "will be to find a hideout in Paris. We'll all go there once the job is done, and take our separate pieces."

"But," Herman said, "we'll be in different parts of the city, with different parts of the castle. Only one group will

17

actually find what we're all looking for. How can we be sure there won't be a doublecross?"

Eustace spread his hands, like St. Francis. "We're all friends here," he said.

There was general skepticism on the faces around the table.

"Very well," Eustace said, with a little sigh for the mistrustfulness of the human mind. "Look about you," he said. "Which of us here would want to spend the rest of his or her life knowing that everyone else at this table was searching for him, with a grudge?"

They all looked around at one another. Now, each face became slightly abashed, as though each had been developing some sort of private plan and now all were having second thoughts. Jean was clearly speaking for them all when he said, "An excellent point, I'm afraid."

"Yes," Rosa said glumly. "It seems we can trust one another."

"Our common interest," Herman said, in a monotone, "must take precedence over selfish desires."

"I hate England," Sir Mortimer said, "but I wouldn't want to have to leave it, not forever. Everywhere else is so much worse."

"Good," Eustace said, and looked around the table. "Any more questions?"

Herman asked, "How much time have we, for preparation?"

"Lida tells me," Eustace answered, "that the dismantling and packing, in far-off Yerbadoro, are nearly finished, and the shipping will begin in three weeks. The parts going by sea will leave first, with the airborne sections coming later. They want the entire castle to arrive in Paris at the same time, ready for immediate reconstruction."

Herman said, "So we have three weeks to assemble our

teams. Thereafter, you will supply us with intelligence as to routes and objectives."

"Exactly."

"With this young lady, Fräulein Perez, as your primary source of this intelligence."

"Through her family and other contacts in Yerbadoro, yes."

Jean, with a little bow in Lida's direction, said, "I pray the young lady will forgive me, but how certain can we be of her information?"

"Years ago I sold guns to her father," Eustace told him. "They're a perfectly reliable family, I guarantee them."

"Ah," Jean said, and offered Lida a semi-tragic smile: "Do forgive me."

Fiery, forceful, flaming, Lida announced, "My father fought the oppressors from the jungles! All his life!"

"Of course," Jean said, taken aback. "Yes."

Eustace looked around. "Anything else?"

The group waited, glancing at one another, but there were no more questions.

"Very well," Eustace said. "You will be hearing from Jean as to our rendezvous point, and we shall meet again in three weeks in Paris, after you have assembled your groups."

❋

After the final guest had departed—Herman Muller, in his open-top black Volkswagen beetle—Eustace turned his eyes, his attention and his hands on Lida. "My dear," he said, in a not quite fatherly way, patting her arm, holding her arm, "success is in our grasp."

"It's wonderful," Lida agreed. "Someday, you shall be a hero of Yerbadoro!"

"But it isn't—exclusively—for Yerbadoro that I'm doing

this, my duckling," Eustace said, drawing the girl a bit closer. "I think you know what I mean."

"Oh, but Eustace," she said, drawing herself a bit farther away, "you know my gratitude can only find verbal expression. I am saving myself."

"Lida—"

"No, please, you kind, generous, brilliant, wonderful, *sweet* man." Now, disengaging his fingers one by one from her arm, she said, "I mustn't tempt you any more with my presence. Good night, Eustace."

Watching the girl go, Eustace continued to smile until she had left the room; whereupon the smile turned rancid. "Saving herself. For what, the Yerbadoroan Army?" Turning to the armoire in which he kept his sherries, he muttered, "Here am I, the premier professional criminal of Europe. I can get into any safe, any bank, any locked room, any strongbox in the world. I can get into *anything*, in short, but her."

2

(a)

Six black taxis muttered and growled at the cabrank just round the corner from London's Dorchester Hotel. It was *not* raining, but neither was the sun shining, and the strollers in beautiful green Hyde Park across the way mostly carried brollies, as did Sir Mortimer Maxwell, swinging his rather jauntily in the manner of a cane as he approached the line of taxis and squinted at each driver in turn. As all six drivers were deeply engrossed in studying the bikini photos in that day's *Sun*, Sir Mortimer's perusal went generally unperceived. Apparently content with what he had seen, Sir Mortimer strolled on to Park Lane and stood there making a lowercase "h" with his umbrella as he smiled across at the park and breathed deep of the bus fumes.

Brreeeett! The Dorchester's lordly doorman accompanied his blast upon the whistle with great vigorous wavings of his arm—a taxi was required, at once, for a Maharajah, no doubt. The first cab left the cabrank, little diesel motor gurgling loud, and curved around to present its right-hand door to the doorman and—a honeymoon couple from Liverpool, temporarily rich from the pools. Ah, well.

21

Sir Mortimer switched his umbrella to the other hand and made a mirror-image "h."

Brreeett-breet-breet! Another taxi was most urgently in demand, and rapidly under way to answer the summons. Sir Mortimer, about-facing on his right heel at the instant of the sound of the doorman's whistle, marched straight to taxi number three—which by attrition had become taxi number one—and entered the passenger compartment.

The driver lowered his paper and lifted his eyes to the rearview mirror: "Yes, guv. Where to?"

"Hel-lo, Bruddy," Sir Mortimer said, with a cheery smile. "Just around the park a bit while we talk."

The driver, Bruddy Dunk by name and plug-ugly by profession, twisted around and looked with surprise—but not pleasure, or displeasure either; merely surprise—at his passenger: "Well, blow me down," he said. "Sir Mortimer himself, in the flesh."

"That's right, Bruddy."

"Let me get it away from here," Bruddy said, and faced front again to put the cab in gear and drive out onto Park Lane, turning left toward Hyde Park Corner.

A small but hard-muscled man of about thirty, Bruddy Dunk had the face of a sport who'd never in his life backed away from an argument but hadn't in every single case won his point. His nose looked like a large peanut, in the shell; his mouth when open revealed tooth gaps wide enough to slip a Ritz cracker through; and his cloth cap appeared to be sewn to his head.

Sir Mortimer waited while Bruddy negotiated the tricky chaos of Hyde Park Corner then took the Carriage Road between the beauty of Hyde Park on the right and the grimness of Kensington Barracks on the left; then he said, "Your sister told me where I'd find you."

"Did she." Something about the manner in which

Bruddy sounded thoroughly noncommittal suggested he was in fact a bit disgruntled that his sister should be bandying his location about.

Sir Mortimer was uninterested in Bruddy's family quarrels. "I thought I might have use for you," he went on, "in a very nice bit of smash-and-grab, but you appear to have turned yourself into an honest cabman."

"Tell the honest truth," Bruddy said, "I stole this cab this very morning."

"In that case," Sir Mortimer said, "why not drive me to my country place while we talk."

"Meter on, or special out-of-city rates?"

"Ho ho," Sir Mortimer said. "You will have your little joke."

❖

Crosshatches of sunlight, Mondrian'd by the struts and supports of the Eiffel Tower, dappled the exhausted tourists walking beneath its splayed legs. Among these, none was more indubitably a tourist or more obviously exhausted—to the point, apparently, of panic—than Andrew Pinkenham. A fiftyish, mild-featured, plumpish man with a distracted manner, Andrew Pinkenham was the very embodiment of the English civil servant, but in fact he was not an English civil servant, he was something entirely different.

However. This seeming tourist, ostensibly exhausted and worried, a putative middle-class civil servant, approached in a tentative and superbly appropriate manner a particular pair of tourists, on whom he'd had his eye for several minutes. These too were quite clearly English, but working class and probably in their forties, a married couple with a shy-but-delighted look to their faces as they gazed about at this foreign soil.

Andrew Pinkenham placed himself diffidently in their path. "I do beg your pardon," he said, "but would you by any stroke of magnificent luck happen to be English?"

The couple looked surprised, though they shouldn't have. "Yes, we are," the man said.

"Oh, thank the good Lord," Andrew said. "I'm at such a loss when surrounded by foreigners."

"Always glad to be a mate to a mate," the man said. "Got to stick together when we're abroad, don't we?"

"Oh, that we do, that we do."

"What's the problem, then?" The man was definitely a take-charge sort, and his wife watched him admiringly.

"I came out today without a farthing," Andrew confessed. "Or a franc, I suppose I should say. Whatever it was, I didn't bring it."

The woman of the pair was instantly sympathetic: "You poor man. You have no money?"

"I'm stony, I'm afraid."

Becoming slightly suspicious, the man now said, "And you want to borrow some, is that it?"

"Oh, good heavens, no," Andrew said, apparently shocked. "I'm no beggar. But if you have the cash to spare, could I possibly write you a check? On my London bank, of course. Nat West."

"A check?" The man's suspicions were not yet entirely allayed. "For how much?"

"Oh, just enough to see me back to my hotel." Carefully gauging the potential resources of the marks, Andrew suggested, "Say, five pounds?"

The man relaxed with a relieved smile. "Oh, I think we could do that," he allowed, becoming expansive, while his wife beamed beside him.

"Wonderful," Andrew said. "I'll just write you out a check here—"

And he did so, leaning against a girder, pausing to say, "To whom shall I make it out?"

"Richard Coe."

"Right you are."

Finishing the check, Andrew waved it in the air a second to dry the ink, then handed it over to the man, who smiled at it, withdrew from his pocket a well-worn wallet, took out a five pound note and handed it over, saying, "And there's your fiver."

"You've absolutely saved my life," Andrew told him, clutching the note.

"Think nothing of it," the man said. "I know how things can be on holiday. In fact, I'm on holiday myself."

Losing interest, preparing to leave, Andrew said, "Oh, really?"

"Yes," the man said. "From Scotland Yard." And suddenly his hand was on Andrew's elbow, and was holding very very tightly. And suddenly the man didn't look such a fool after all. He was brisk and purposeful as he said to his wife, "You go whistle up a gendarme, love, while I keep an eye on this chap."

"Right," she said, and *she* was brisk and purposeful too, as she hurried off.

Andrew, his heart simultaneously sinking and rising into his throat, sputtered and spluttered: "What? Really, you— Surely you don't think—"

"Yes, well," said the man, "we'll sort it all out at headquarters, won't we?"

"But— I can't think why you'd— But—"

Andrew was on the very brink of abandoning pretense, was in fact seriously considering kicking this officious officer in the knee and trying to make a run for it (though he was dreadfully out of condition and hadn't run in thirty years or more), when suddenly a new person appeared, and it was with utter astonishment that Andrew realized he was looking at the mangled face of Bruddy Dunk. Also, that Bruddy was dressed as a chauffeur. And finally, that Bruddy was saying words to Andrew—Andrew did his best to listen.

What Bruddy was saying was as follows: "Yes, sir, the car's waiting right over there."

Car? Waiting? But before Andrew could ask any stupid questions, Bruddy turned his ugly-but-calm face toward the policeman, frowning at the check still held in the policeman's free hand (the hand not holding Andrew's elbow). "What's this?" Bruddy said. "Borrowing from strangers, sir?" And he plucked the check right out of the policeman's hand, making it disappear immediately inside his chauffeur's jacket, while at the same time saying, "No, sir, not while I'm around."

"See here!" the policeman said, letting go of Andrew in his agitation. "Give back that check!"

"You go to the car, sir," Bruddy told Andrew calmly, "while I sort this out."

Gratefully Andrew backed away.

"Here, now," the policeman said, pointing at Andrew. "You just stay where you are."

Bruddy moved, stepping between the policeman and Andrew, saying, "That's five pounds, isn't it, sir?" And from an inner pocket he withdrew a wallet every bit as old and disreputable as the policeman's had been.

"Just a minute now," the policeman said.

"In the first place," Bruddy told him, now sounding just as hard and brisk and sure of himself as the policeman did, "you're no more a copper this side of the water than I am. And in the second place, you don't have the check. Now, you want the five quid or not?"

Bruddy held out a five pound note under the policeman's nose. Andrew watched the play of thought and stratagem and frustration cross the policeman's reddening face, until finally the man said, "Garrrr!" and snatched the five pound note out of Bruddy's hand. "I'll remember your face," the policeman threatened.

"Gord," said Bruddy, "I'll do my best to forget yours." And he turned away, shooing Andrew ahead of himself to an illegally parked long black Daimler limousine.

After which, it was hardly a surprise at all to Andrew to find Sir Mortimer Maxwell waiting for him in the back seat.

(b)

Renee Chateaupierre, the most beautiful cat-burglar in Cannes, with the longest slenderest legs and the blackest sleekest hair and the quickest lightest fingers in her profession, helped herself to all the sparkling jewelry while the movie producer snored atop his snoring starlet. Oddly enough, her snores were deeper in tone than his, but together they made a fairly pleasant harmony. Monotonous, though.

It was also strange but true that his jewelry was more extensive and richer than hers. The starlet had been good for merely a few pairs of earrings, a broach or two, a necklace, a few other trinkets, but from the movie producer Renee had accepted rings, a platinum identification bracelet, a gold watch inset with rubies, a gold money clasp in the shape of a dollar sign (plus all the money it clasped), several valuable sets of cuff links, and a silver cigarette lighter.

And now she was finished, without ever having made enough noise to disturb the lovers at their snoring. Moving in swift slender silence, Renee crossed the room to the window through which she had entered and smoothly slid across the sill.

The ledge was narrow, but so were Renee's feet. Ignoring the rather magnificent view of the Mediterranean, Renee glided across the front of the wedding-cake-white hotel, a dark shadow in the pre-dawn empty night, passing dark windows toward the one—leading to an empty room—which had been her route on arrival.

Four windows from that goal there came a sudden change in Renee's direction. An arm snaked out from the darkness of this open window, wrapped itself around her lithe and slender waist, and yanked her off her ledge, through the opening, and into the darkness.

Renee, naturally, opened her mouth to scream, but before she could do so a hand smelling not unpleasantly of Canoe after-shave firmly pressed itself against the lower half of her face, barring her from making any vocal noise at all.

Or breathing, in fact, since the hand covered her nose as well. And the other arm was still about her waist. Kicking, gasping, writhing, struggling, clawing at the hand against her face, Renee found herself inexorably drawn into the dark room and across it, farther and farther from the safe rectangle of the window, until she was abruptly spun, lifted, and flung upon a bed. "Oof!" she said, tried to get her elbows under her so she could rise, and her attacker dropped his entire body on top of her, crushing her onto the mattress. "Oof!" she said once more, then quickly gulped in air and yelled, "Help! Police!"

"Don't be silly, Renee," said the calm, seductive, very familiar voice in her ear. "You don't want the police any more than I do."

Startled, recognizing the voice but not yet able to unite

it with a name or face, Renee stopped yelling and said instead, "What?"

The man lifted part of his weight from her onto his elbows—so at least he was a gentleman. Then he reached out to the bedside lamp and switched it on, and Renee, blinking in the yellow light, saw above her the smiling and well-remembered face of Jean LeFraque. "Hello, my love," he said.

"Jean!" Forgetting all other distress, Renee said, "What are *you* doing *here?*"

Seductively grinning at her, moving his lower torso just a bit, Jean said, "I have business to discuss with you, my sweet."

Renee made a head gesture to indicate the bed. "This isn't my business."

"Surely," Jean said, his hip rotation becoming more pronounced, "we can be comfortable while we chat."

Renee did a thing involving her knee, which Jean didn't at all like. She could tell he didn't like it by the way his face became all scrinched up and lost all its color, and by the way he sagged between his supporting elbows, and also by the way he offered no protest when she rolled him off her onto the other side of the bed, saying, "Let's be *un*-comfortable."

Renee, free at last, got to her feet and smoothed down her black cashmere sweater and narrow black cotton pants. Meanwhile, Jean remained on the bed, curled like a shrimp.

Renee was standing in front of the mirror, fluffing her hair, when Jean finally uncoiled himself and sat up, moving slowly, like a weary old man. Moving painfully to the edge of the bed, cautiously lowering his legs over the side, he said, "Renee, you never did have any sense of humor."

Looking at him in the mirror, Renee offered him a mock-sympathetic smile, saying, "Poor sweetheart, did I hurt you?"

"Only temporarily, thank God."

Renee turned, saying, "I'm glad to hear it. I'm ready to listen now."

Jean looked at her, and she could see him considering the possibility of prolonging his agony in order to get some sympathy—which might eventually lead to what he'd had in mind in the first place—but then she saw him realize she was the wrong person for such a ploy, and she knew their platonic relationship had been re-established when at last he shrugged and said, "Fine. To business."

*

The Bistro Chagrin was crowded tonight, though it was a Thursday. This working-class joint in Montmartre, just off Pigalle, attracted a very tough, very laconic, very fatalistic clientele, who didn't give a damn if it was Thursday or not. What matters, eh?

Above the droning din of existential conversation drifted the notes of a piano, playing over and over a vaguely slow but syncopated, catchy yet boring, reminiscent yet not quite plagiarized little tune. The piano itself, in a far corner of the long crowded smoky room, was a battered upright, concealing from general view the man playing it. Charles Moule was his name, he was short and and slender but wiry-tough, he was of indeterminate age somewhere shy of forty, and he had a long bony deeply lined face with a smoldering cigarette dangling from the corner of his mouth and with blank eyes that spoke of too much hope blighted in too many bistros on too many Thursday nights. And Tuesdays as well.

The fight broke out shortly after eight. The two men at a table in the middle of the room suddenly lunged at one another, swinging haymakers. The two women at the same table leaped to their feet, dragging daggers from the rolled tops of their stockings and having at one another. One of the men, struck by a flailing fist, stagged backward into another table, knocking a customer's beer into the customer's lap, and in no time at all the fight had spread into a general melee. Punches were thrown, and so were glasses, bottles, knives, chairs, tables, and the occasional waiter.

And through it all, the piano tinkled. Protected by the wall of the upright piano, lost in his own thoughts, Charles Moule played on, oblivious of the screams, the curses, the threats, the moans and groans of the wounded, the crashing of furniture, the smashing of glass, and ultimately the EE-OO EE-OO of approaching sirens. The same little tune babbled endlessly on, the same cigarette smoldered in the corner of Charles's mouth, the same faraway reflection remained in his blank eyes.

Police burst in, swinging their nightsticks. They made order, but they did so by first making even more chaos—the old omelet-egg idea. But it didn't take them long to dampen the enthusiasm of the combatants, and then to start moving the ambulatory outside to paddy wagons. Ambulances arrived to deal with the non-ambulatory, and very soon the Bistro Chagrin was quiet again, except for that infernal tune. Waiters crept out from the safety of the kitchen to right the tables and chairs, sweep up the debris, restore order. The bistro settled into a kind of exhausted empty pensiveness, and Charles played on.

Which was when Jean LeFraque and Renee Chateaupierre arrived, drifting as though aimlessly into the joint, ordering Pernod (for Renee) and cassis (for Jean), then drifting past the empty tables to the upright piano, leaning their elbows and their glasses on the piano top, looking over it down at Charles. It was Jean who said, "Hello, Charles."

31

Charles looked up, with a sad little smile, then looked down again at his moving fingers. The piano played on.

Renee spoke: "Hello, Charles."

Not looking up, Charles said, "Hello, Jean. Ah, Renee, good to see you back."

"I wasn't gone anywhere," Renee said.

"C'est la vie," said Charles, with a small shrug of one shoulder.

Jean said, "Mauron told me you were here."

"The piano is a good thing," Charles said, "when you want to be alone with your thoughts."

Looking around the empty room, Renee said, "Not much business."

With another small shrug, Charles said, "Well, it's a week night."

"True."

"We had some action before."

Getting down to business, Jean said, "Listen, Charles, you want in on something big?"

Charles shrugged. "Naturally," he said.

"Come on, then."

Charles seemed to consider. The piano played on. At last Charles shrugged, saying, "All right, why not." Then he said, "Renee? Would you help me?"

"Any time at all, Charles," she said.

Charles nodded at the sheet music open on the piano stand. "Would you turn the page?"

"Of course."

Leaning over the piano top, Renee turned the page. Charles, squinting at the new page of sheet music, brought the tune to an end. "C'est fini," he said, and got to his feet.

(c)

On a narrow canal branching off a less narrow canal branching off a fairly wide canal branching off the Grand Canal of Venice, a gondola came sliding along, with a singing gondolier. He didn't sing particularly well, but at least he knew all the words. In Italian.

Two people reclined within the gondola. One was a nice lady from Ohio, and the other was Angelo Salvagambelli, who was not particularly nice at all. They were smoodjing together, these people from two different worlds, murmuring sweet nothings into one another's ear.

From the opposite direction came a flat-bottomed rowboat, effectively blocking the route of the gondola through the canal. In the rowboat, strongly rowing, sat Rosa Palermo, who didn't stop her strong rowing until her boat actually crashed into the prow of the gondola, bringing the gondola to an abrupt stop and hurling the gondolier into the dubious water, which brought the gondolier's song also to an abrupt stop.

The nice lady from Ohio and Angelo Salvagambelli both stopped smoodjing and stared into one another's eyes, taken aback. Simultaneously, they said, "What was that?" Simultaneously, they answered, "I don't know."

Rosa, getting to her feet in the rowboat and brandishing a long heavy oar, now yelled at the top of her voice, "*Worm!*"

The nice lady from Ohio and Angelo Salvagambelli both sat up and stared at this threatening apparition. Astounded, Angelo said, "Rosa?"

"*You,*" Rosa answered. "Our children are starving, our furniture is in the street, and where are *you?*"

"Rosa," Angelo said, "what the hell is *this?*"

The nice lady from Ohio stared at Angelo: "You're *married?*"

Gesturing at Rosa, Angelo cried, "To *that?* What do you think of me?"

The gondolier at last surfaced and attempted to scramble back up onto his perch at the rear of the gondola, shouting. He continued to shout and continued to scramble, but no one paid him the slightest attention.

The nice lady from Ohio said, "No, Angelo. I can't stand a liar."

"*Me?*" Angelo was thunderstruck.

"Good-bye, Angelo," the nice lady from Ohio said. "Good-bye, forever." And with that, she dove into the dreadful water of the canal and swam strongly away, using the stroke she'd learned in Red Cross class.

Angelo watched her go, his mouth open. The gondolier continued to try to scramble up onto the gondola, and continued to shout. He continued to be ignored.

Angelo turned his head to stare at Rosa. "Rosa," he said. "You did this to me. Rosa, what are you pulling?"

"I want to talk to you, Angelo," Rosa said, putting down her oar and no longer shouting. "I'm in a hurry," she said, in a brisk and practical way. "It's a business proposition."

"If I *would* get married," Angelo told her, "I'd marry my grandmother before I'd marry you."

"What you do in your family is up to you, Angelo. I want to talk business. Get out of that boudoir and into my boat."

"Join *you?* If you think I'd—"

"Get out of there," Rosa said, picking up the oar again, "or I'll sink it."

Angelo was nothing if not clearheaded; he knew when he was beaten. Reluctantly transferring himself from the gondola to the rowboat, he complained, "You couldn't wait till we were finished? Just a little longer? Do you realize that was a *schoolteacher* from Canton, Ohio? Do you realize they have a *union,* schoolteachers in America? Do you realize she was going to buy me a *watch?*"

Unsympathetic, Rosa sat down, reinserted the brandished oar into its oarlock, and said, "You listen to me, Angelo, you'll be able to buy your own watch. And someone nice to wear it." She began to row. The gondolier scrambled and shouted. Angelo sat gingerly in the prow of the rowboat. The canal smelled awful.

*

The occupant of the jail cell, Vito Palone, was a retired master criminal, a bent little old man with a large gray head and a long gray nose and tired gray eyes. His cell was fairly small but not at all uncomfortable, with pretty curtains on the barred window and a nice rectangle of carpet on the floor, fluffy pillows and blankets on the bunk, pictures on the walls, a small bookcase, even a hot plate and tiny refrigerator. Seated in a comfortable vinyl chair at a small but adequate writing desk, Vito Palone was writing his memoirs, in a small neat hand, in ink, on lined paper. At the moment he was writing:

"It was then, in 1954, that I entered upon my final period of honest endeavor. With my profits from the burglaries described in chapter seventeen, I opened a small manufacturing concern, specializing in bones of the saints and fragments of the true cross. We made the fragments of the true cross in three different sizes, each encased in its own cube of clear Lucite plastic. Interestingly enough, our domestic sales were heaviest in the smallest size, while the largest size made up the bulk of our foreign sales, particularly to Ireland. In fact, years later many of these plastic cubes containing the fragments of the true cross were thrown at British soldiers during the troubles in Belfast. So once again I had made a small contribution to history. Taxes, however, ate up most of the profits of my factory, and in early 1955 I was forced to close my doors. Determined to get my money back from the tax officials, I . . ."

At this point in his narrative, Vito Palone was interrupted by the removal of the outer wall of his cell. The whole thing, masonry, brick, mortar, was ripped off the face of the building and crumbled away in a great cloud of dust and rumbling of material. Vito, terrified, leaped to his feet, overturning his chair and table, and backed quacking to his door, as far from that now nonexistent wall as he could get.

And through the new opening, with its cloud of dust and smoke, stumbled two creatures, both in black clothing and black knit caps, both wearing crash helmets and scuba-diving equipment and thick work gloves.

Vito stared in horror. "Martians!" he screamed. "Help, it's Martians!"

One of the Martians lifted its scuba mask and revealed the irritated face of Rosa Palermo. "What Martians, you idiot?" she demanded. "It's me, Rosa Palermo. And here's Angelo, Angelo Salvagambelli, you remember him."

"Rosa?" Vito peered at her through the descending dust.

"Yeah, sure. Rosa. What do you think?"

"Rosa." Then, in a swift transition from terror to indignation, Vito cried, "What have you done to my wall?"

Lifting his own scuba mask, Angelo said, "We're here to rescue you."

"Rescue?" Vito stared at these two crazy people in their crazy clothes. "Who wants to be rescued?"

But they wouldn't listen to him. Replacing their scuba masks, they approached and each took one of his arms. "Come on," Rosa said, her voice muffled by the mask. "We'll explain the details later."

"Let me go! Let me go!" Vito struggled uselessly against the strong younger hands.

They drew him inexorably toward the ruined wall of his ruined cell, trampling on the fallen pictures of the saints. "Vito!" cried Angelo, hearty and stupid. "Vito, it's your comeback!"

Vito wailed as they dragged him out to the sunlight: "But I don't *want* to come back!"

Who listens?

(d)

The factory safe was being expertly broken into by Rudi Schlisselmann, a fiftyish, irritable, big-mouthed professional burglar. Around him, the city of Dortmund slept the sleep of honest burghers. Beneath his fingers, the safe's combination lock went click-click-click, as the tumblers whispered to him their secrets.

And then the lights went on, *pop*, just like that, and two uniformed policemen rushed into the office, clutching automatics. Rudi leaped to his feet, clutching his chest: "My heart!"

They ignored him. "Stop where you are, Rudi Schlisselmann!" shouted the first.

"We have you this time!" shouted the second. "It's jail for you!"

"But—" Rudi stared frantically from cold face to cold face. "Friends!" he cried, inaccurately. "Wait! Wait!"

But they wouldn't wait. Without ceremony, they hustled Rudi out of the office and down the long room past all the lathes and out through the door Rudi himself had so recently and so expertly jimmied, while Rudi continued to shout his useless appeals. "Fellows," he cried, "I'm a veteran! I was in the Wehrmacht! We guys in uniform have to stick together!"

Nothing. No response. No help. The bastard cops were probably too young to even remember the Wehrmacht. In fact, all of a sudden *everybody* was too young to remember the Wehrmacht.

Outside was the police car, the same shade of dusty green as the policemen's uniforms, with its bright blue flasher light on top and black letters spelling POLIZEI in a white rectangle on each door. The policemen were just hustling Rudi into the vehicle when another policeman came along, obviously an officer, definitely bad-tempered, thoroughly in charge. "So," said this officer, tall and thin and stern-looking, "you caught him."

"Yes, Herr Oberleutnant," said the first policeman, snapping to attention.

"Caught him in the act," said the second policeman, "Herr Oberleutnant," also snapping to attention.

"Very good," the officer said, approving of them with slight nods. "Very good."

They preened under this minimal praise, shifting about as much as a person can do while standing at attention.

"You will be commended for this," the officer went on, with more slight brisk nods, and the policemen's cheeks swelled with pleasure. Then the officer said, "I'll take over now. Bring him to my car."

"Yes, Herr Oberleutnant."

"Yes, Herr Oberleutnant."

Rudi, meanwhile, had stopped his useless shouting and wheedling and was staring in a glazed panicky disbelief at the officer. He didn't even resist when the two policemen marched him down the dark block to the black Mercedes under the next streetlamp, where the officer gestured curtly at the back seat and said, "put him in."

They did so. The rear window was open, and Rudi immediately stuck his head out into the light of the streetlamp, looking up in open-mouthed wonder at the officer, who told the policeman, "Return to your beat, now. Good luck."

"Thank you, Herr Oberleutnant."

"Thank you, Herr Oberleutnant."

With stiff salutes, the two policemen marched quickly away to their own car, got in, and drove off, while the officer continued to stand on the sidewalk watching them and Rudi continued to hold his head outside the car window, staring up at the officer's chiseled face. Finally, as the police car was leaving, Rudi said, in soft tentative wonder, "Herman?"

Herman continued to watch the police car on out of sight.

Half whispering, Rudi said, "Herman Muller?"

"Just wait," Herman said. "They may circle the block."

"I've always liked you, Herman," Rudi said, with an endearing big smile. "You know that, don't you? I've always said you were a prince. Ask anybody. I talk about you all the time. 'That Prince,' I say. 'Herman Muller, he's a Prince.'"

"Hush, Rudi."

"The uniform fits you nice. It's beautiful on you."

At last Herman was satisfied that the police were gone. Swiftly he got behind the wheel of the Mercedes and started the engine. Rudi leaned forward to rest his forearms on the seat back and say, "We don't see enough of each other."

"Oh, we will, Rudi," Herman told him, as they drove away. "We'll see a *lot* of one another."

*

Deep in the Black Forest was the Lederhosen Inn, the world's largest cuckoo clock, a baroque but beautiful explosion of turned wood, stag antlers, alpenstocks, beer steins, banners, and general *Gemütlichkeit,* practically all of it authentic. Out in front of the inn waited four huge chartered buses, all with banners on their sides proclaiming: "Sons of the Mountains 23rd Annual Hike and Picnic." And from inside the Inn came the sound of a male chorus, strong joyful sounds emerging from hundreds of rugged male throats, belting out "I Am a Happy Wanderer."

Within the inn, however, were no rugged male throats belting out any song at all. A rugged phonograph was playing a *record* of hundreds of rugged male throats belting out "I Am a Happy Wanderer," at one end of a large high-ceilinged ballroom packed with trencher tables. Packed at these trencher tables were hundreds of fifty-five-year-old fat men in lederhosen, all of whom gave the appearance that they'd been drinking beer steadily for a month. They were now somnolent, comatose, moribund; in a word, passed out. They looked like the result of a gas attack.

All but one. Moving in the room was one man, and one man only. Otto Berg by name, he looked like all the unconscious men, and was dressed like all the unconscious men, but he was different. First, he was different because he was up and awake and moving around and sober. And second, he was different because he was picking everybody else's pockets.

This was probably the biggest drunk-rolling caper in recorded history. There was an open knapsack on Otto Berg's back, and as he moved among his sleeping benefactors he tossed a steady stream of watches and wallets and rings into this knapsack, which was becoming quite significantly heavy.

Suddenly, out of the corner of his eye, Otto saw movement other than his own. It was the heavy end door of the ballroom, next to the record player, slowly opening. At once Otto dropped onto the nearest open bench space and pretended to be unconscious. When he ceased to move, in these circumstances, he became to all intents and purposes invisible.

The heavy door finished opening, and in came a hesitant, tentative, reluctant Rudi Schlisselmann, dressed as a waiter in black tails and white shirt and black bow tie, and carrying a tray of beer mugs. Trying to look in all directions at once while a panicky placatory smile flickered and disappeared and jolted across his face, Rudi crept through the room, whispering, "Otto? Otto?"

No one could have heard such whispering in a room full of that chorus of happy wanderers, and no one did hear it, including the man whose name was being mentioned. That is, he didn't hear it until one of Rudi's whispered "Otto"s came at the same instant the male chorus on the record was taking a breath. Also, Rudi was at that time very near the feigning Otto, and this combination of chorus pause and propinquity made Otto hear his name being whispered, which made him look surreptitiously around, which made him see Rudi passing by, which made him sit up and whisper, "Rudi!"

Unfortunately, the chorus was in full voice again, having replenished its breath, and Rudi heard nothing. Otto had to get to his feet and follow Rudi and tap Rudi on the shoulder. Then he had to wait while Rudi juggled the tray full of beer mugs, as he'd been startled out of his wits. But the tray didn't get away from him, the beer mugs didn't fall, the crash didn't awaken all the neighbors asleep at their places, and Rudi and Otto were not at once torn limb from limb by a lot of fifty-five-year-old fat men. Instead, Rudi managed to keep the tray under control, and to keep himself under control as he turned around and whispered, "Otto! *There* you are!"

"Rudi? What are you doing *here?*"

"I've got the local Volkswagen franchise," Rudi whispered acidly. "What do you think I'm doing here? Come on, will you, my arms are falling off." And he put the tray down on a nearby table.

"Come on?" Otto was having trouble catching up. "Come on where?"

"With me, naturally."

"But I can't leave yet," Otto whispered. "I'm not finished."

Rudi gave him a look of scorn. "What do you want, their shoelaces? I'm here with Herman Muller, I'm talking about something big."

Otto looked around, rather regretfully; then shrugged. "Oh, well," he said. "It's an annual affair, I can finish next year."

3

The Hotel Vendôme, on the Rue de la Paix in Paris's First Arrondissement, is for those delicate few who find the Ritz garish. With a broadly sweeping but very dark lobby so thoroughly swathed in broadloom and brocade that the entire revolution of May 1968 took place outside without a single sound penetrating so far as the second rank of potted palms, the clientele is assured that absolutely no reminder of the twentieth century will ever disturb their slumber. Unless, of course, the management makes the mistake of letting a room to the wrong person; a possibility lessened by the outrageous prices charged.

But no system is foolproof. Consider:

It is early afternoon. Gently suspiring bodies, sodden with lunch, sag on all the low sofas. Gentle snores flow soothingly from beneath walrus moustaches. The principal light source is the diamonds worn by most of the female guests. A waiter in a maroon Eton jacket crosses, carrying a mint julep on a silver tray; not a sound emanates from the contact of his shoes with the thick carpet, swirling with art deco design. Then, with a faint shushing sound, an elevator door slides open—the amenities are twentieth century, even if nothing else is—and all hell breaks loose.

Her name was Maria Colleen San Salvador Porfirio Hennessy Lynch. She was the wife of Escobar Diaz McMahon Grande Pajaro Lynch, El Presidente of Yerbadoro, and she didn't care who knew it. An explosive woman, with voice and gestures larger than life, she had the self-confidence and determination of the bull on first entering the ring. Larded with makeup, draped with layer upon layer of the most expensive clothing Paris could offer, she wore Incan jewelry hanging around her like scaffolding around a cathedral. She had never had second thoughts about anything, had never failed to get her way, and had only the slightest suspicion that in fact other human beings actually existed.

She entered the Vendôme lobby from the elevator under full sail, striding purposefully forward and bellowing at the top of her voice. "—*never* going to get my hair done if all we do is look at *lots* day in, day out!"

Shock! Turmoil! Spasms! Snores became snorts, red-rimmed eyes opened in astonishment, and several of the most active tenants even considered getting to their feet. Maria, unknowing and uncaring, continued both to stride and to shout: "If today's barren field is as hopeless as yesterday's barren field," she announced to all of the First Arrondissement, "I am *through* looking at barren fields!"

In her foaming wake trailed five men, four of them trotting and smiling and bowing, one of them strolling and smiling and nodding. The stroller was Maria's husband, El Presidente Lynch himself, a tall and handsome man, with a handsomeness that was at first appearance rugged but on closer examination merely decayed. Self-indulgence and cleverness showed in his full-lipped smile, in his sardonic eyes, in the casual ease with which his careless stride kept pace with everybody else's bustling haste. As for the four bustlers, two were Yerbadoroan bodyguards, one was an official of the International Exposition Board, and one was a functionary from the French Government. They, and the Lynches, were here to find a site for the expected castle, and Maria for one was growing bored with the problem: "If the truth be told," she roared at the lobby, shaking dust from the wall sconces, "I like that goddam building right where it is."

Her husband's smile glinted in the musky lobby. Softly, he said, "You'll like it better in Paris, Maria."

His voice, particularly in comparison with hers, was the barest whisper, the slightest hint of sound; nevertheless, she faltered for a second, her expression becoming for just an instant uncertain. Then she smiled again, confidence renewed. "I'm sure I will!" she sang out, and sailed through the outer doors to the waiting limousine, the five men following after.

✿

The "goddam building" was, in fact, a goddam castle, called Escondido Castle, and it stood at present in pretty parkland by the Yerbadoro River, twenty miles north of Enfermedad City, the capital of the nation. Not quite two hundred years old, Escondido Castle had been built by one of those Irish freebooters who had taken over Yerbadoro from the Spanish back in the eighteenth century, and the design had been influenced both by the owner's memory of stately homes in his native Ireland and by his work crew's memory of Incan temples in the nearby jungles. The result was essentially pleasing, here and there surprising, and perfectly acceptable as a castle, though somewhat smaller than the word "castle" might suggest. In fact, the outbuildings and the wall around the courtyard would remain in Yerbadoro—and would look rather odd all by themselves—while only the main structure, a compact three-story building of large gray stone blocks, would be dismantled and shipped to France.

*

Today's barren lot was a winner. Even Maria had to admit it, at the top of her voice: "You know, I like this spot."

"I'm glad, my dear," her husband said.

It was in fact a very pleasant spot, fairly high on a hill in Montmartre, the only truly hilly part of Paris. Narrow twisty streets, old buildings, and here a rectangular vacant lot where an old ruined factory, once an absinthe distillery, had recently been torn down. "Yes," Maria said, turning in a slow circle, looking about her and nodding, "I think I could live here."

"Visit," Escobar Lynch corrected, with a small warning smile.

"That's right," Maria said. "Visit. I think I could visit here." Turning to the two Frenchmen, she said, "It's a deal. You boys have sold a lot."

4

Here and there in the bustling center of Paris underground garages have been built—dug? constructed? scooped out?—with access direct from the wide busy streets. The hustling little vehicles of Paris descend into these nests without slackening their street speed, so that to an innocent bystander on the sidewalk it looks as though every once in a while a hurrying automobile is simply swallowed up into a hole in the ground. Zip zip zip, go all the cars, and then zip-*floop*. Zip, zip, zip, zip-*floop*, zip zip, zip-*floop*, all day long. It can become unnerving, at least to innocent bystanders who continue to stand there all day long instead of going on about their business.

On a sunny Tuesday, at midday, such a bystander would have seen, amid the other zipping beeping traffic, a black Volkswagen beetle convertible with the top down, looking like a midget command car, sporting front and rear the oval white license plates of West Germany. Driving this VW and yelling at the nearby French drivers in German, was Rudi Schlisselmann, burglar extraordinary. Beside him, munching morosely on pills to aid dyspepsia, sat Otto Berg, the last of the happy wanderers. And seated ramrod straight in back, looking to neither left nor right, suffering the cacophony of the traffic as he would suffer any fools—that is, only up to a point—sat Herman Muller, team leader.

Zip-*floop*. Volkswagen all gone.

Shortly thereafter, if our bystander were still standing by, he would have seen a little red Fiat zipping among the blue and white Renaults and Simcas, and at the wheel of the little red Fiat he would have seen Angelo Salvagambelli, teeth sparkling in a lush smile, black hair glistening in the wind, a white polyester scarf wrapped in devil-may-care fashion around his neck. Beside him, blinking in terror at the traffic and the noise and the people and the sunshine, cowered Vito Palone, retired master criminal dragged out of retirement by popular demand. Or at least by demand of Rosa Palermo, who was now squeezed uncomfortably into the small back seat of the Fiat, from which command post she kept up a steady stream of advice and warning to Angelo in re the other traffic, all of which Angelo cheerfully ignored.

Zip-*floop*. Ta ta, Fiat.

Almost immediately after that, our loitering bystander's attention would have been attracted to the smallest, oldest, most battered and dented little gray Renault ever seen on the streets of Paris. Since its license plate began with "75," the number code for Parisian cars, this bedraggled little Renault must frequently have been seen on the streets of Paris, and it's only a wonder the dogcatcher never grabbed it. Alone at the wheel of this mutt—for who could possibly be induced to travel anywhere in it other than its driver? —slouched Charles Moule, pianist and existentialist, a cigarette smoldering from the corner of his mouth.

Zip-*floop*. A *bas*, Renault.

After a few minutes of no activity, our bystander— doesn't he have a home?—next sees coming along the street sailing gaily through the traffic, a bicycle built for two, with Jean LeFraque in front and beautiful cat-burglar Renee Chateaupierre in back. This bicycle, with its attractive riders, being taller, more slender and more agile than most of the other traffic, was not only attracting a lot of attention from the other travelers but was also making better time.

Zip-*floop*. Away the bicycle, accelerating.

But what's *this* coming? A London taxicab, in Paris? Naturally, with everybody's pal but nobody's fool Bruddy Dunk at the wheel. And reclining in comfort in back, feet stretched well out, were Sir Mortimer Maxwell and Andrew Pinkenham, discussing Great Crimes of the Century.

Zip-*floop*. To the depths, Austin taxi.

Our bystander, convinced that he'd seen everything, departed at last, but he was wrong. One more vehicle now came down the same street, growling mightily and cutting left and right through the slower traffic; a motorcycle, with sidecar. At the handlebars of the motorcycle, head sheathed in leather goggles, perched Eustace Dench, master criminal, the singular begetter and deviser of this entire caper. And in the sidecar, startlingly beautiful and windblown, the Yerba-doroan lovely, Lida Perez, for whom—perhaps—this whole enterprise was being undertaken.

Zip-*floop*. Motorcycle *and* sidecar down the ramp.

Down the ramp, down and down the ramp, curving down through the gray concrete tunnel of the ever descending ramp, past parking levels filled with sleeping autos, past deeper parking levels only half filled, past deeper parking levels with merely a vehicle here and a vehicle there, until at last the motorcycle, with sidecar, reached the very bottom of the ramp and emerged onto the lowest level of all, where there were no parked cars at all.

Oh, yes, there were. In the farthest farthest corner, half hidden beyond all the concrete support pillars, were clustered the black Beetle, the red Fiat, the doomed Renault, the now-riderless bicycle built for two, the taxi (with its orange *To Hire* sign alight over the windshield), and their twelve various drivers and passengers. Eustace steered his motorcycle to this group—or these groups, as the nationalities seemed to be bunching together and avoiding strangers —and brought it to a racketing stop. Climbing off the motorcycle, removing his goggles, Eustace stepped forward to the group—or groups—with a confident smile, saying, "Well. We're all here. Time to get started."

Vito Palone, the poor old man, had no English. He said, in Italian (the only language he had), "What was that?"

Eustace frowned at him: "What?"

Charles Moule, existential though he might be, had neither English *nor* Italian, so it was in reference to what Vito had said to Eustace that Charles said to Jean LeFraque, "What did he say?"

"Just a minute now," Eustace said, with down-patting hand movements, as though trying to quell a mutinous mob. He was feeling it start to slip away, and he was determined it wouldn't happen. "Let's get organized here," he said. "Let's just be calm and get organized."

Otto Berg, whose happy wandering had been mostly limited to Germany and who spoke none of the languages bandied about so far in this parking level, now said to the group at large, "Would *somebody* tell me what's going on?" In German.

"Nobody's making any sense!" poor old Vito cried, growing excited.

Eustace, also growing excited, yelled back at Vito, "Why don't you speak English?"

"He's Italian," Rosa said.

"*You're* Italian," Eustace pointed out. "*You* speak English."

50

"Reluctantly," she said.

Sir Mortimer now stepped forward, saying, "Come along, Eustace, let's get started, shall we?"

A babble of voices demanded to know what had just been said, by whom, to whom, in what language, and why. Eustace, dropping back a pace, stared at them all in growing horror. *None* of them except the team leaders spoke English.

*

Three hours later. Eustace, in rolled-up shirt sleeves, was exhausted and depressed and even pessimistic, and much the same expression could be seen on all the faces around him. With endless translations and backtracking and misunderstandings and sketches in the dust on the various vehicles he was now *fairly* sure he'd managed to communicate his plan to all these monolinguals (he was monolingual himself, Eustace was, but since his one language was English it didn't matter), but by the time his rather complicated and tricky plan had been fully laid out in this manner he'd begun to lose some of his delight in it. Maybe the plan wasn't any good after all, maybe it was exactly as bad as it had begun to sound somewhere in the second hour of explanation.

No; that couldn't be so. He was a planner, was Eustace Dench, a magnificent planner. He simply had to have faith that, before being faced with all these blank faces and mulish dispositions, the plan he'd devised *had been* a good one. And would be a good one again.

"Right, then," he said, forcing himself to straighten up and appear at least slightly determined and optimistic. "We've all gone over the plan together."

"We've-all-gone-over-the-plan-together," dutifully and

dully droned Rosa and Herman and Jean, each in his or her own language.

Eustace sighed. "We've ironed out our differences," he said.

"We've-ironed-out-our-differences," thudded the translations.

"We've agreed on payment."

"We've-agreed-on-payment."

There was general grumbling. The question of shares had made for some trouble a while back.

Well, it wouldn't make for trouble now. "We *have* agreed on payment," Eustace said sternly, glaring around. There were no translations this time, but none were needed; and there was no more grumbling either, so Eustace went on: "We all know what we're supposed to do."

"We-all-know-what-we're-supposed-to-do."

Trying for a pep-talk ring to his voice, Eustace said, "So now, let's go do it!"

"So-now-let's-go-do-it."

5

The rain poured down, it lashed, it drenched, it fell in sheets and buckets and cascades, it plunged down from the sky as though God, having just finished His bath, had pulled the plug on the celestial tub. The port city of Southampton squatted fatalistically beneath this deluge, its entire citizenry remaining sensibly indoors. At the harbor, the freighters moved sluggishly at their moorings, the sea pockmarked with raindrops, the ships' decks awash with water. Puddles widening into lakes lay on the cobblestones and blacktop of the harbor. The clouds were dark and low, almost touching the funnels of the freighters, and the roar of the rain blotted out all other sounds.

The taxi from London came nosing hesitantly through the puddles, along the harbor quay. At the wheel, Bruddy Dunk grumbled to himself and squinted out the windscreen, past the hard-working but virtually useless wipers. Here and there along the quay piles of cargo lay stacked, some beneath tarpaulins, some exposed to the pelting rain. At each of these mounds Bruddy paused, while Andrew Pinkenham in the back seat peered through the water-streaming side window trying to read whatever ownership or destination information might be imprinted on the cargo.

"Trust bloody Sir M," Bruddy grumbled to himself, as he paused at yet another anonymous mountain of cargo, "to absent himself when the discomfort starts."

Andrew, leaning forward toward the open side of the glass partition between front and back seats, called, "What say?"

"Nothing, man, nothing. What about this lot, then?"

"A moment." Andrew's nose pressed to the side window, he closed one eye and squinted the other, and read aloud, "Egyptian Air Force."

"What's that?"

"Egyptian Air Force!"

"Not ours, then," Bruddy said and drove on to the next. "Bloody girl's bloody information probably all wet anyway," he muttered. "Wet as bloody us."

"What say?"

"Nothing, by bloody Christ, nothing! Mind your own business, can't you?"

"No need to get shirty," Andrew said.

"Shirty," Bruddy muttered. "Bloody— How about this, then?" And he paused at a great sprawling stack of wooden crates, each covered wtih stenciled words.

Once again, Andrew pressed his nose to the side window, but this time before he could read anything his own exhalation of breath steamed the window.

Bruddy called, "That it?"

"I don't know," Andrew said, rubbing the steam off with the sleeve of his Burberry. "Impossible to see in this rain."

"Open the bloody window."

"Afraid I'll drown," Andrew said. "You didn't by any chance drive off the end of the pier without noticing, did you?"

"Arf, arf," said Bruddy. "Open the bloody window and let's get this over with."

Even placid Andrew was getting a bit short-tempered in this weather. "What are *you* in such a hurry for?" he demanded.

For once, Bruddy didn't take offense. Instead, he treated the question seriously, and gave it a serious answer: "I'm in a hurry," he explained, "to go someplace dry and warm and drink something wet and cold."

"Amen, Bruddy, amen."

"So open the bloody window and read the bloody boxes."

"If I must, I must."

Andrew tugged down the window, and at once the rain poured in. So did the thunderous roar of the rain. Face pinched up against the flurry of cold raindrops, Andrew looked out at the crates and read *Escondido Castle— Property of Government of Yerbadoro.* "That's it!" he cried.

Bruddy, frowning at him in the rearview mirror, yelled over the rain, "What say?"

Andrew pushed the window up, lessening the volume of rain in more ways than one. "That's it," he said, and shivered. "Now, let's go to the place you mentioned for the reason cited."

"Done and done," said Bruddy.

◦

In the sunshine, high on a hill overlooking the port of Livorno, Rosa Palermo and Angelo Salvagambelli stood beside the little red Fiat, Rosa looking through binoculars, watching the cargo from the South American ship being loaded into two large orange trucks. Beyond the ships the Ligurian Sea glistened and sparkled in the sunlight, and up from the city came the plink and tinkle of mandolin music. The air was warm, the sun bright, the hill green, the day thoroughly beautiful, and Angelo was growing impatient. "Rosa," he said.

She made no reply, but went on looking through the binoculars at the lading going on below.

"Rosa," Angelo repeated, "let me look."

"There's nothing to see," Rosa said, and went on looking herself.

"If there's nothing to see," Angelo said, reasonably enough, "stop looking and let *me* look."

"In a minute," Rosa said.

"Rosa . . ."

"Be quiet, I can't see."

Angelo's boredom and impatience led him to push the issue. Tugging at Rosa's arm, he said, "Rosa, it's my turn!"

At once, Rosa exploded into a counterattack, leaping away from him as though his arm-tug had been some sort of karate chop.

"You're so domineering!" she yelled, glaring at him. "A woman can't breathe around you! Always grinding women beneath your heel!"

Astounded, Angelo fell back against the side of the Fiat, as though utterly felled by this unjust accusation, and feebly pointed at his own chest, as though to say *Me?*

"Yes, you!" Rosa told him, and pointed her own finger at his chest. "You and only you!" Then she thrust the binoculars at him, crying, "Here! You'll pull them out of my hands, *here* they are!"

Moving away from the Fiat, turning his back, flinging his arms this way and that to express rejection and despair, Angelo said, "I don't want them. I don't care to look."

"You'd knock me down to get them," Rosa insisted,

following him away from the car. "You'd break my arm! Here, here, here they are, I submit!"

Spinning back to face her, his expression furious, Angelo cried, "Submit? To rob a man of his manhood is your only pleasure!"

Now it was Rosa's turn to fall back in astonishment, clutching at her chest. "I? *I?*"

"You! You!"

The argument continued for some time.

●

Night. The two orange trucks with the shipment from South America ground slowly up the twisting road through the Swiss Alps. Behind them buzzed the black Volkswagen beetle convertible, top up. Rudi Schlisselmann was driving, while Otto Berg beside him thoughtfully chewed a sausage sandwich. Herman Muller was not along on this ride.

Otto broke a long silence by breaking wind. Then he sighed. Then he yawned, showing a lot of half-chewed sausage sandwich. Then he swallowed, scratched himself, and said, "Well, Corporal, we're back in operation together again."

Smiling, watching the trucks slowly gaining ground ahead of him up the mountain, Rudi said, "Like the good old days."

"It's good to be working with the Major again."

"Especially," Rudi said, "considering some of the other meatballs in this job."

"You know what the Major says," Otto reminded him. "No enterprise of any scope can be accomplished without allies."

With a sly grin, Rudi said, "At least for a while, eh, Sergeant?"

Chuckling heartily, Otto said, "Until the objective is attained, Corporal."

Both had a good laugh at that. Rudi, the first to sober, frowned again through the windshield, saying, "Still. To be on a job with the Italians again. It gives me a creepy feeling."

Sternly opposed to any expression of doubt, Otto said, "The Major knows what he's doing, Corporal."

Not entirely convinced, but obedient, Rudi nodded: "Oh, I know that, Sergeant. I know that."

❉

The boat train from London to Paris travels overland as far as Dover, where the freight cars and passenger cars and wagons-lits (or sleeping cars) are placed on a ferry, a huge bulky awkward-looking ferry with one lower deck as lined with railroad track as any freight yard. The English locomotives and dining cars are left behind (good!), and the ferry pushes drunkenly off toward Calais, where French locomotives (not so good) and dining cars (very good) will be added for the overland run to Paris.

Sir Mortimer Maxwell had hoped to have the tiny wagon-lit compartment to himself, but he turned out to have a roommate—or cellmate. What was worse, this cellmate was an obese Frenchman without English. What was even worse than that, this obese Frenchman without English was accompanied by an entire hamper of food—bread, wine, sausages, cheese, fruit—from which he fed his fat face *constantly*. And noisily. Chomp chomp, squgg squgg, slish slish. It was simply not to be borne.

The fact of the matter was, Sir Mortimor didn't much like to travel by either train *or* boat, and traveling by both simultaneously did nothing, in his opinion, to improve either. He was sitting in an extremely cramped train compartment, listening to a fat Frenchman gnaw his way through the world's food supply, and the extremely cramped train compartment was weaving and rolling like a ship. It was damned unpleasant.

It was finally more unpleasant than Sir Mortimer could bear, and he left his short narrow wagon-lit bed, donned a dressing gown, and left the compartment. Staggering down the narrow corridor to the end, he left the car, turned right, found an open door, and went down the steps to lean out and look at all the railroad cars stacked in here like toys in a child's dresser drawer. Far above was the yellow-painted steel ceiling, spaced infrequently with rather dim light bulbs. And over there, glimpsed between other railroad cars, were the two yellow freight cars which were Sir Mortimer's special interest. He nodded at them, as though greeting an old acquaintance. He was happy to see them, but not at all happy at where they had brought him.

Oh, well; it was all for a good cause. And someday it would all be over, and he could return to Maxwell Manor well supplied with the cash necessary to keep the world at bay. In the meantime, stiff upper lip. He would soldier on.

And for this moment, he would sit upon these steps here and contemplate that glimpse of yellow freight car. It was more comfortable—and more reassuring—than the compartment full of eating Frenchman.

*

But not every wagon-lit compartment was disturbing to its occupants. In one not terribly far from Sir Mortimer's, in the rolling darkness, two voices were speaking, both coming from the bottom bunk. One of the voices belonged to Charles Moule, the other to Renee Chateaupierre, and both voices vibrated softly with repressed emotion. "Then," Charles was saying, "after Claudia was shot by the tourists in Barcelona, life no longer seemed worth the effort."

"You don't have to talk about this, Charles," Renee said.

"But I feel I must, Renee."

"It's not necessary, Charles."

"It's necessary to *me*, Renee. After—after what has happened between us, I can no longer remain silent. Tonight is my rebirth. I want you to undestand my soul."

"I do understand your soul, Charles."

"Do you understand how I felt after Barcelona?"

"But you could never show it," Renee said.

"How could I show it?"

"You never could."

"I could never show it."

❖

It was raining at Le Bourget, the oldest and smallest of Paris's three airports, the one where Lindbergh landed after his transatlantic crossing. The London taxi parked by the fence gleamed darkly wet in the sheets of rain. Within the taxi were Bruddy and Andrew, and Bruddy was saying, "Doesn't it ever stop raining? When this job is done, I'm taking my share and traveling the world over till I find—"

"There!" said Andrew, pointing toward the distant runway. "That's it!"

"What? Oh ho, you're right."

The two men watched the cargo plane landing—a DC-3, painted in the Yerbadoroan colors of purple and black. Squish squish, went its wheels on the runway. Rapidly the plane shushed by, spray flying.

"Easy," Bruddy said, beneath his breath. "Take it easy, old son, don't wreck that plane."

"Right on time," Andrew said, happily smiling at his watch. "That girl Lida's information is infallible."

Bruddy wasn't yet ready to fall over into total optimism. "Just let the rest of it work as well," he said. "And let it bloody well stop raining."

6

In her simple hotel room on the Rue des Ecoles, Lida prepared herself for her solitary bed. In a floor-length white cotton nightgown that clearly exhibited both her beauty and her strength of character, she was about to climb into the narrow bed and switch off the light, when there came a knock at the door.

She hesitated. Who would be knocking at the door at this hour? A lone girl, defenseless in a hotel room in Paris, must ask herself such questions.

The knock was repeated.

Well. Even a lone girl, defenseless in a hotel room in Paris, must be allowed a certain curiosity. And if the door of the hotel room is locked, which this one most certainly was, there was perhaps not *too* much risk in responding to a knock on it by voicing one's curiosity aloud. Emboldened by these reflections, Lida tiptoed to the door, leaned close to it, and was about to speak when the knock occurred a third time. This knock, coming when Lida was bent close to the door, was so loud in her ear that she started back with an involuntary cry, her small right fist pressed to her chest between her breasts. She waited, wide-eyed, gazing at the door, but when nothing further happened she dared approach it again, and this time she called, "Who is it?"

The voice from beyond the wood was one she had never expected to hear again in this life: "Manuel," it said.

Manuel! Joyfully, Lida unlocked the door and flung it open. "Manuel!"

Manuel entered, shutting the door behind himself. A sturdy handsome peasant with a broad nose and a grim, glum manner, Manuel was dressed in rough corduroy trousers held up by a length of rope instead of a belt, a pair of heavy workshoes, and a coarse cotton shirt with a wide collar and flaring sleeves. "Lida!" he said, his voice hoarse with emotion, and held his arms wide.

Lida flew to them. They embraced, passionately, murmuring endearments to one another in Spanish, the native tongue of Yerbadoro and in fact the only language with which Manuel was at all familiar.

After the first embrace, Lida and Manuel held one another at arm's length, gazing at one another, drinking one another in. Speaking in Spanish, so that Manuel could understand her, Lida said, "Oh, Manuel! I had given you up for dead."

"Even death could not keep me from my swan, my Lida," said Manuel, who in his own language was some shucks.

"Manuel," Lida asked, "how did you escape the terrors of El Presidente?"

"The jungle befriended me," he explained simply. "I had many adventures, and have at last found my way to Paris, and to you, my beloved."

"My heart!"

"My life!"

"My all!"

"My own!"

Again they flung their arms around one another, but before they could continue with whatever had been their intentions a discreet tapping sounded at the door.

Instantly, Manuel was suspicious. Pushing Lida from himself, glaring like a bantam rooster at the door, he said, "Who is that? What man is that?"

Frightened, innocent, Lida told the truth: "I don't know."

But an instant later she did know, because it was clearly the voice of Eustace that sounded through the door, calling in that hoarse voice peculiar to people who are trying to shout without speaking loudly, "Lida? Are you decent?"

Manuel bristled. "A male!" he said.

Trying to calm him, Lida whispered, "It's my benefactor, Eustace Dench. I told you about him."

"Lida?" Eustace's hoarse voice sounded again. "Are you awake, dear?"

Switching to English, Lida called, "Just one moment, please." Then, reverting to Spanish, she told Manuel, "I have told him you are my cousin."

"Cousin?" Twice as suspicious as before, Manuel glowered upon his true love. "What hanky-panky is this?"

"I wasn't sure he would help me," she explained, "if he knew I was betrothed. Besides, I thought you dead." Then, hastily, she added, "Though I never gave up hope, of course."

With another tapping at the door, Eustace called again: "Hurry, Lida. Hurry."

"Be good now," Lida warned Manuel, worried. "And you're my cousin. We need the assistance of these people."

Manuel growled, but despite the truculence of his face, Lida could see he would go along.

Tremulous, Lida at last opened the door, and Eustace entered, wearing a red smoking jacket and carrying a bottle of champagne in one hand and two glasses in the other. Lida closed the door, and the broad smile on Eustace's face disappeared when he caught sight of Manuel. Eustace stared at Manuel, who stared at the champagne.

"Hello," said Eustace, in a tone of unwelcome surprise. "And what have we here?"

"My cousin," Lida told him. "Miraculously restored to life."

"That," Manuel said, in his South American Spanish, "is an alcoholic beverage."

"I take it," Eustace said, "this is another one who doesn't speak English."

"Sadly, no," Lida agreed. "Manuel has no English." Then, in Spanish, she made the formal introduction: "Manuel Cornudo, may I present Eustace Dench." Back in English, she said, "Eustace Dench, my cousin, Manuel Cornudo."

Manuel sullenly but manfully stuck out his hand. Eustace dithered a bit, not quite sure what to do with the bottle and glasses. In a sullen monotone, Manuel said, "I am very pleased to meet you."

Eustace extended the champagne bottle toward Lida: "My dear?" She took the bottle from him, and he took Manuel's horny hand, gesturing with the hand holding the two glasses. "How do you do," he said. "Any cousin of Lida's is a cousin of mine. Welcome back from the dead."

As they continued to shake hands, Manuel gazed grimly at Eustace and said, "How would you like me to punch you in the face?"

"Charming," Eustace said, released Manuel's hand, and turned to Lida to say, "I take it we're going to put up with —put—that is, put your cousin up."

65

"Oh, that's very kind of you," Lida said, as there came a sudden brisk knocking at the door.

Manuel bristled: *"Another* lover?"

"Manuel," Lida cried, "how can you say such a thing? You know I have always been true to you."

"Even when you thought me dead?"

The knocking was repeated at the door, this time accompanied by the loud whisper of Angelo, calling in Italian, "Lida? My heart? Are you there?"

Eustace frowned. "That sounds like Angelo."

Fitfully, Lida handed the champagne bottle to Manuel and opened the door. Immediately, in bounded Angelo, with a huge smile, a big bottle of red wine, and a couple of glasses. His smile wrinkled like a snake when he saw the other two men.

"Yes, indeed," Manuel said, gazing at the bottle of wine and struggling toward sarcasm. "I have heard that one should not drink the water."

Eustace, apparently deciding a stern manner was the best way to survive this experience, turned on Angelo, saying, "Well, Angelo? May I ask the meaning of this?"

Ignoring Eustace, turning the full mellifluous power of his Italian upon Lida, Angelo said, "I feared you might have given your heart to another, but I had no idea you entertained groups."

To Manuel, Lida explained, "This is Angelo. He doesn't speak Spanish."

"He doesn't need to," Manuel said bitterly.

Turning to Angelo, Lida said in her halting Italian, "Thank you. But. Tired. Me."

Disillusioned, Angelo said, "Well, that's only to be expected."

Retaining the social niceties of her convent upbringing,

66

though distractedly, Lida made the introductions: "Manuel, Angelo. Angelo, Manuel."

Manuel stuck his hand out as though he wished there were a knife in it. Angelo fidgeted briefly with bottle and glasses, then handed the bottle to Lida and shook Manuel's hand.

Said Manuel, in Spanish, with a tight smile, "May the dogs tear your heart out."

Said Angelo, in Italian, with a tight smile, "May your mother get the mange."

There came another knock at the door. Lida raised imploring eyes to heaven.

"The United States Marines, no doubt," Eustace commented.

Speaking in English, Lida said, "I really wish none of this would happen."

Dazedly, she handed the wine bottle to Manuel, who stood there holding the two bottles as though they were Indian clubs and he was about to go into his act. Lida opened the door and in strode Rudi, carrying a bottle of Rhine wine and two glasses. Before noticing the other men, he said, in his native German (what else?), "A preliminary celebration, eh?" Then, seeing the other three, he stopped dead, saying, "What's this, a lineup for Interpol?"

Fatalistic, Lida closed the door, while Manuel stared at her. "I cannot believe," he said, "that you have taken up with a German."

In desperate Spanish, she told him, "I haven't taken up with anyone!"

Gesturing with the champagne and red wine bottles, Manuel said, "You seem to have taken up with everyone!"

Rudi glowered at Manuel. "A Spaniard," he commented inaccurately. "I thought I told you to wait in the ditch."

"Why does no one speak English?" Eustace asked plaintively. "It's such a pleasant language."

Hopelessly, Lida made the introductions: "Manuel, Rudi. Rudi, Manuel."

Rudi fidgeted briefly with his bottle and glasses. then handed the bottle to Lida, who was already reaching for it, not even bothering to look, knowing it was coming. With grim correct politeness, Rudi stuck his hand out toward Manuel. Manuel was about to respond, then noticed his hands were now full of wine bottles. He glared at them, glared at Rudi, glared at the wine bottle in Lida's hand, glared at the two wine bottles in his own hands, then suddenly reared back with the champagne bottle, obviously planning to let Rudi have it across the head; launching him, as it were.

General consternation. Rudi leaped into a defensive stance, a wine glass in each hand. Angelo nimbly skipped to one side, while Eustace and Lida both rushed forward, shouting, "No! No!" With Eustace and Lida standing in front of Manuel, waving their arms over their heads to keep Manuel from advancing on Rudi, everybody yelled at once, in all the languages available, Manuel threatening blood-curdling revenges on every male in Paris, Angelo insisting upon his noncombatant status, and Rudi declaring himself ready to take on whole battalions of Spaniards, bring 'em on, he'll wipe up the floor with them, and so forth. When finally everybody paused to take a deep breath, the blessed silence was broken by the sound of somebody knocking at the door.

Everybody in the room looked at everybody else in the room. "No more," Lida said, first in English and then in Spanish. "No more."

"Enough," Eustace said, "is very definitely enough."

Formally handing one glass to Angelo and one glass to Rudi, he marched across the room, flung open the door, and Rosa marched in.

Everybody stared from Rosa to Lida.

"Oh, now!" Lida said. "Now! this is *too* much!"

Rosa, hands on hips, glared in brief silence around at each man in turn, then began to speak. In English, she said, "Are you idiots trying to wake the whole hotel?" Then, in Italian, she demanded of Angelo, "Can't you take even a *small* vacation from lechery?" Before Angelo could answer, she rounded on Rudi, snarling in glib if heavily accented German, "Don't try to behave as though you were passionate. We all know you're German." With both Angelo and Rudi becoming apoplectic, she turned to Lida and said, with a gesture at Manuel, "And this one? Does he have a language?"

"Spanish," Lida said. "He's my cousin Manuel. From Yerbadoro."

With a gesture at the two bottles in Manuel's hands, Rosa said, "Your cousin has a drinking problem." Then, turning to Manuel, she said, in quick harsh Spanish that sounded like sleet landing on a tin roof, "You will ruin your liver if you drink all that." Pointing at the bed, she told him, "Now, go to sleep. We'll talk in the morning."

Manuel looked stunned. "But—"

"Never mind," Rosa told him, and turned on Eustace. In English, she told him, "You and your Musketeers also. To bed. Your *own* beds."

"Rosa, I assure you—"

But she wasn't listening. To Lida, she said, "You come with me. You'll stay in my room tonight, where you'll be safe, away from these grandfathers."

Lida, too taken aback to argue, permitted Rosa to

hustle her from the room; on the way out, she handed Rudi back his wine. Then she and Rosa were gone, and the men were left alone.

Rudi was the first to react; with a bitter attempt at indifference. "Actually," he said, "I prefer blondes." And he marched from the room, head held high.

Angelo was next. "I am very happy," he announced, to no one's comprehension but his own, "that I have not understood a word that anyone has said." With which he started toward the door, stopped, went back, took his red wine back from Manuel, and at last departed.

Eustace approached Manuel, who had the glazed look of a man who's just had a chandelier fall on him. Plucking his champagne bottle from Manuel's unresisting hand, Eustace said to him, with bright and angry irony, "Welcome to Paris. Delighted to have you." And Eustace too exited, in as dignified a manner as possible, closing the door behind himself.

7

Alone in Lida's room, early next morning, Manuel sat blinking on the edge of Lida's bed, not knowing what to do next. He had slept, he had awakened, he had dressed himself, and now he was sitting here, hands dangling between his knees. He had not eaten for some time, and he was hungry, but if he left this room would he ever see Lida again? On the other hand, if he *stayed* in this room would he ever see her again? They were very strange people, those new friends of hers. The presence of the loud woman with the impressive bosom had reassured him somewhat as to the sexual respectability of the relationships, but they were still very strange people. And they all seemed to drink a great deal.

A knock at the door.

Manuel look at the door. He squinted at it. Another thing these people did a lot of was knocking at doors. Never in his whole life had Manuel met such people for knocking at doors. If he were around these people for very long he would no doubt develop unpleasant symptoms from all this knocking on doors; a tic, perhaps, or a tendency toward hunched shoulders.

Another knock at the door.

Possibly the most sensible way to live among such people would be to keep all doors open at all times. Or would they knock on the doors anyway? Manuel had seen motion pictures made in North America in which people— usually the "secretary" of the "boss," whatever any of that meant—knocked on open doors as an indication of their intention to cross the threshold. Possibly these people would do the same. Possibly they were all secretaries.

A third knock at the door.

Manuel sighed; he practically groaned. Getting to his feet, he crossed the room and pulled open the door merely to stop that person out there from knocking on it any more, and LIDA WALKED INTO THE ROOM!

"*Lida!*"

"Manuel," she said briskly. She was all business this morning.

Manuel wasn't. Manuel was all lust this morning, at least toward Lida, just as he had been last night. "My love!" he cried, and slammed the door again, regardless of future knockers.

"At last we can talk," Lida said.

"At last we can make love!" Manuel cried, trying to crush her in his embrace.

Pushing him away in a distracted inattentive manner, she said, "I'm serious, Manuel."

"So am I," Manuel said, the words and expression heartfelt.

But Lida was simply too involved in her own thoughts and plans to notice. Glancing worriedly toward the door— afraid, no doubt, of people knocking—she said, "I don't know how much time I have."

Nor did Manuel. "Lie down," he said. "Hurry."

"Manuel, listen to me," Lida said. "These are dangerous people."

Ready to crack up, his hands trembling, Manuel said, "I can be dangerous too, my dove."

Would *nothing* attract the woman's attention? She said, "I don't trust them."

"You can trust *me*," he said. His fluttering fingers stroked her cheek, her arm, the swell of her breast.

Annoyed, distracted, baffled, Lida pushed all those hands away: "What are you *doing*?"

But Manuel would not be stopped. The bed was behind her, and he was moving inexorably forward, struggling, puffing, muttering low: "I was—lost in the jungle. I thought I'd never—see you again."

"Why, Manuel! Do you—? My *dear*!"

At last, he had attracted her attention.

*

Once again, Lida's mind was on business. Naked, beautiful, but all passion at least for the moment spent, she strode back and forth past the foot of the bed in the small room, while an exhausted Manuel sat propped against the headboard, breathing.

"We have to make a plan," she said.

Manuel nodded his weary head: "Yes, my love."

"I don't trust these people."

"Yes, my love."

"They've promised me half the money, but I don't believe them."

"They're crooks," Manuel said, trying unsuccessfully to rouse himself to indignation.

"Well, I had no choice in that," Lida said, reasonably

enough. "Crooks were the only people who could help me."

"That's true," Manuel said.

"But we have to watch them," Lida said. "All the time, every second, until we regain the people's money."

Manuel nodded some more. "Yes, my love."

"Alert at all times," Lida said.

"Yes, my love," Manuel said and, still nodding, he fell asleep.

"We must be prepared for treachery at any instant," Lida said, then noticed that Manuel's eyes were closed, his body relaxed, his mouth open, and his breathing regular. She frowned at him. "Are you asleep?"

Manuel gave the only possible affirmative answer to that question—none.

"Oh, Manuel," Lida said. "I need you. I—"

A knock at the door.

Manuel opened bleary eyes. "It's the secretaries," he said. "The secretaries are back."

"Hush," Lida told him, and stood silently looking at the door.

And now Eustace's voice sounded through it: "Lida? Are you in there?"

Lida hesitated, then called, "Yes. I'm here."

The doorknob rattled, but just before their lovemaking Lida had locked it. Eustace called again: "It's time to go."

"Just one moment," Lida called, then turned to Manuel. "You must help me, Manuel," she whispered urgently. "You're the only one I can trust."

"Oh, you can trust me," Manuel said. His thirty-second nap had refreshed him, and a gleam was returning to his eye.

"Later, Manuel," Lida said. "We'll have—time. Later."

74

8

Driving up the Boulevard Raspail toward the Pont de la Concorde, in a new white Renault freshly stolen by Vito Palone, were Vito himself with Rosa Palermo and Angelo Salvagambelli. Rosa was driving, with Angelo in the passenger seat beside her and Vito in back, grumbling. "I was happy in my retirement," Vito was saying.

"You were in jail," Rosa reminded him.

"I was in retirement," Vito insisted. "I had my flowers. I was writing my memoirs."

Interested, Angelo half turned in his seat, asking, "Memoirs? Am I in them?"

Spiteful, Vito shrugged, saying, "A footnote, only."

Hurt, Angelo said, "After all we've been though together?"

Rosa, glancing in the rearview mirror, said, "What was this footnote about?"

Vito said, "That Greek sailor we kidnapped from the British lord."

"What?" Angelo stared. "You put that in the book?"

"Of course."

"Don't!" Angelo cried. "Take it out at *once!*"

"Now you don't want to be in the book."

"If you put me in the book like *that*," Angelo told him, "you'll put me in jail."

With an offhand wave, Vito said, "So you're out of the book."

Heartfelt gratitude in his expression, Angelo said, "Thank you, Vito."

"Think nothing of it."

Rosa glanced at her companions, seemed to have it in mind to say something, and then seemed to think better of it. She shook her head, and steered the Renault across the Pont de la Concorde, around the Place de la Concorde, and northwest up the Champs Elysées.

✽

On the Boulevard Périphérique, the elevated highway ringing the city line of Paris, Herman Muller stood at an overpass, watching the endless traffic rolling northward toward the city. From time to time he looked at his watch, and betrayed his impatience only with a slight frown.

Similarly, when at last he saw the two large orange trucks coming his way, his reaction was no more than a thin smile, quickly gone. He walked at an easy pace to the on-ramp, watching the trucks grind heavily up the ramp, and showed another brief thin smile when the Volkswagen appeared behind it, top down, Rudi driving and Otto sitting next to him. The Volkswagen stopped at the top of the ramp and Herman vaulted over the side and into the back seat. Pushing a walkie-talkie out of his way, he settled himself back there as Rudi drove out onto the highway, following the orange trucks.

"Hello, Major," Otto said.

"Sergeant. Any difficulty?"

"None," Otto said.

"Good." Herman leaned back, permitting himself yet another smile. "A fine day," he said. "An excellent day for a tactical exercise."

As he finished speaking, the walkie-talkie on the seat beside him piped up, in a tinny approximation of Eustace's voice: "Group A? Come in, Group A."

Herman glanced at the walkie-talkie, first in surprise, and then in some amusement. "Group A," he repeated. "That's us." Picking up the walkie-talkie, he pressed the button on its side and said, "Yes, yes, here we are."

The tinny voice said, "Where are you, Group A?"

"In the automobile," Herman said, with exaggerated exactitude. "On the Boulevard Périphérique. Behind the trucks."

"Are you on schedule?"

"As a matter of fact, no," Herman said. "But then, the drivers of those trucks don't know about *our* schedule, do they? I would say we are approximately twenty-five minutes late."

"Well, it can't be helped," said the tinny voice, in a brave manner.

"Very true."

"Well, anyway," the tinny brave voice said, "I'm in position now. Keep in touch."

"Without a doubt," Herman said, and put the walkie-talkie down as though it were a three-day-old fish.

*

In Ménilmontant, in the London taxi parked on a narrow side street, Sir Mortimer and Bruddy and Andrew were having a discussion concerning a number of profound subjects: loyalty, finance, personal security. Bruddy was saying, "The rest of them would bloody well take the whole thing, if *they* found it."

From the walkie-talkie on the front seat next to Bruddy came the same tinny voice that had spoken to Herman. This time it said, "Group B. Come in, Group B."

Bruddy, ignoring the interruption, went on talking: "If we find the lolly," he told Andrew and Sir Mortimer, "*I* say we do the lot of them just the way they'd do us."

"Group B? Come *in*, Group B."

Bruddy picked up the walkie-talkie, apparently considering the discussion at an end, but Sir Mortimer said, "Wait, now, Bruddy. Don't answer that yet. Let's sort this out first."

"It's sorted," Bruddy told him. "Far's I'm concerned it is."

"Group B? Can you hear me, Group B?"

Thoughtfully, slowly, considering each separate word, Andrew said, "I must admit, Sir M, I do lean toward agreement with young Bruddy."

"I do not intend," Sir Mortimer said firmly, "to spend the rest of my days in hiding. I *like* Maxwell Manor."

"Then take it with you," Bruddy suggested. "Like this bloody twit's castle from South America."

The tinny voice, clearly becoming desperate, sounded again from the walkie-talkie: "Group B, what's wrong? *Do* come in, Group B."

"I'd better answer this thing," Bruddy said, picking up the walkie-talkie, "before the bloody man has a stroke."

"This discussion," Sir Mortimer said, "is not over."

"Right, right," Bruddy said carelessly.

"Group *Bee*-eee! Where *are* you?"

Bruddy pushed the button on the side of the machine, and spoke. "Keep your trousers buttoned, here we are."

The tinny voice expressed delight and relief: "Bruddy! *There* you are!"

Bruddy, his voice dangerously soft, said, "The idea of the group numbers was, we wouldn't be mentioning anybody's name."

"Oh!" said the tinny voice. "I *am* sorry!"

"Aff a mo," Bruddy said, and turned to the two in the back seat. "Time for you to hop it."

"Right you are," said Andrew.

"This discussion," Sir Mortimer insisted, "is still open."

"Right, right," Bruddy said.

The two older men got out of the cab, as the tinny voice, nervous again, said, "Bru-uh. B. B? Group B?"

"You almost did it again," Bruddy said, watching Andrew and Sir Mortimer walk off in different directions.

"Oh, no," the tinny voice assured him. "No, I won't. I wouldn't."

"That's good," Bruddy told him, and added, "We're all fine here."

"That's fine, then. Fine. Signing off."

"Right," said Bruddy, and released the button. "Twit," he said.

✻

Jean LeFraque, leaning against a boxcar in the freight yards behind the Gare de la Chappelle, heard his jacket pocket speak to him, in a tinny voice. "Group C," it said. "Come in, Group C. Are you there?"

Jean took the walkie-talkie from his pocket, and replied: "*I* am here. My group has not as yet arrived."

"They're not? Is something wrong? Shouldn't they—"

"Wait," Jean said. "Something coming in now."

A switching engine was approaching, bringing a long

string of cars, including several wagons-lits. If all had gone well, Renee and Charles would still be in one of those wagons-lits, having hidden while the other passengers made their departure. Farther down the long string of cars were two bright yellow freight cars.

"Hello?" asked the tinny voice. "Group C? Hello?"

"Yes," Jean said. "Here they come now. My group, and the objects of our attention."

"Ahhhh," said the tinny voice. "Superb."

"You echo my sentiments," Jean told him, and smiled as he watched the wagons-lits go by.

❖

In the compartment in which the reborn Charles had been opening his soul to Renee, the bunks were now both closed into their recesses in the wall, and yet from the bottom bunk the voices still rose, as in a ghost story. The voice of Renee was saying, "Then, when my affair with my uncle came to an end—"

"Wait," said the voice of Charles, and the closed bunk opened slightly. "Isn't that the freight yard?" asked the now-louder voice of Charles.

"Is it?" Rustling sounds ensued, and then Renee's voice again. "So it is."

The voice of Charles said, "I'll never forget this journey with you, Renee."

"Nor I with you. I too am reborn. It was—wonderful, Charles."

"Wonderful."

"Wonderful."

But now—" The sigh of Charles was heard. "Life calls."

❖

The white Renault circled the Arc de Triomphe. Then it circled it again. Then it circled it again. A thousand cars a minute came roaring and beeping and skidding and racing into the Place Charles de Gaulle, entering from the Avenue Kléber or the Avenue Victor Hugo or the Avenue de la Grande Armée or the Avenue Foch or the Rue Lauriston or the Avenue Carnot or the Avenue MacMahon or the Avenue de Wagram or the Avenue Hoche or the Avenue de Friedland or the Avenue des Champs Elysées or the Rue Vernet or the Avenue Marceau or the Avenue D'Iéna or the Rue La Pérouse. Then they all went dashing and spinning around the Arc de Triomphe, only to shoot away again down any one of those fifteen avenues and streets, leaving only the white Renault continuing to circle. And circle. And circle.

Rosa, with the wheel locked in a permanent half-turn to the left, spoke through gritted teeth: "I can't stand this much longer. They're half an hour late."

"They'll be along," Angelo said. "We knew it wasn't a matter of split-second timing."

"I should have had you drive," Rosa said, "regardless of how bad you are at it."

"Bad? I?"

"Ptchah," Rosa said, for answer.

The walkie-talkie in the storage space under the dashboard suddenly spoke: "Calling Group D. Are you there?"

'And now *him*," Rosa said. Keeping one hand on the wheel, maneuvering through the crazy flow and flash of traffic hurtling around the Arc de Triomphe, she picked up the walkie-talkie and said, "Yes, we're here."

But the walkie-talkie was not reassured. "Group D?" it asked. "Where are you? Are you there?"

Push the button; now she remembered. Pushing the button, she said, "Where would I be? Of course I'm here."

"There you are!"

"But where's everybody else, that's the question!"

"On their way," the tinny voice promised. "I spoke to them, and they're on their way."

"Good," Rosa said, as a Simca cut too sharply in front of her, and she avoided an accident only by cutting too sharply in front of a Morris Mini. Horns sounded, as usual.

So did the walkie-talkie. It said, "Are you all right there? Is everything all right? Everything running smoothly?"

Utterly ensnarled in fast-moving traffic, Rosa had neither the attention nor the patience to go on chatting with a walkie-talkie. Dropping it into Angelo's lap, she said, "Here, you talk to him."

*

Eustace was on the hotel roof, alone, seated in a folding chair at a folding table. On the folding table were several maps, various sheets of paper, a thermos jug of tea, some pens and scratch pads, and four walkie-talkies, each boldly lettered in white paint: A - B - C - D. A and B and C were on the table now, but D was in his hand, and the voice that came from it was suddenly not Rosa's voice at all, but an entirely different voice, speaking an entirely different language.

Eustace didn't know it yet, but the new voice belonged to Angelo, and what he was saying, in Italian, was, "What do you want now?"

"Who's that?" Eustace demanded. "Who's talking there?"

"Why don't you leave us alone," the walkie-talkie asked him, in a language he didn't understand, "and let us do our work?"

Fiddling with the walkie-talkie dial, Eustace muttered, "What is this? What have I here, Radio Free Europe?"

"Why don't you talk Italian," demanded the walkie-talkie, in Italian, "like a civilized man? Like Michelangelo. Like all the Popes."

With sudden suspicion, Eustace said, "Angelo? Is that you?"

And now Rosa's voice came back, harsh, irritable, impatient, saying, "Go away, Eustace! We're busy!"

"No names!" Eustace shouted. There was no response to that at all, so more gently he said, "I'm only trying to keep things organized." Still no response. Sadly, he shook his head and put the walkie-talkie down on the table with the others. "We had the empire *such* a long time," he said. "You'd think *someone* out there would have learned English."

9

Three men were on duty in the freight yard switching office behind the Gare de la Chappelle when their door opened and Jean LeFraque entered, his arm around the charming shoulders of Renee Chateaupierre. Renee was exquisite in flowing scarves and loose blouse and slim slacks, while Jean was thoroughly distinguished in his dark vested suit and narrow black tie and narrow black hat. Beyond the three workers were the large plate glass windows with their panoramic view of the freight yards, including—just to the left; see them?—the two yellow boxcars.

There's a reason why confidence men are called *confidence* men; they exude the stuff, as did Jean now, approaching the three workmen, smiling with absolute self-assurance, saying, "All right, men, carry on. This isn't an official inspection."

The three men hadn't thought it was. They had, in fact, assumed that Jean and Renee were merely tourists, civilians, lay persons who had inadvertently gone through one of those *No Admittance—Authorized Personnel Only* doorways with which all our lives are so thoroughly circumscribed. But

clearly this was not the case. If this self-assured and confident gentleman in a three-piece suit and narrow black tie
was telling them his presence was *not* an official inspection,
the inference was clear that his presence *could be* an official
inspection. Meaning that he must be an official. Which
while it was not exactly an explanation of his presence—
and certainly not an explanation of the beautiful lady's
presence—did more or less soothe the three workmen's minds
with the idea that some sort of explanation was possible.

And forthcoming. Jean went on, "I'm just showing the
young lady around." Hugging Renee even tighter, smiling
down on her fondly—and a bit lecherously—he added, "Let
her see how things work."

Wide-eyed, Renee looked at the three men. "The
trains are so *big*," she said, in the tiny sexy-innocent voice
of the utterly depraved little girl.

And now the three workmen understood; or at least
thought they understood. Armed with this information—
or misinformation—all three relaxed and began to smile, both
in complicity with Jean and in pleasure at Renee.

*

The usual state of the traffic entering and circling and
leaving the area of the Arc de Triomphe is perilous in the
extreme, but the situation was just about to get much worse;
hard to believe. Nevertheless, it was true, and it all began
when the two orange trucks we have seen before growled
and slouched their way amid the Simcas and Citroëns, up
from the south and out onto the dizzy circle surrounding the
arch. Little did the drivers of those trucks know, but their
presence was the cue for several other actions to commence.

The first of these was that Rosa Palermo took her foot
off the accelerator. "And there they are at last," she said,

ignoring the banshee wails of horns behind her prompted by the Renault's loss of momentum. "Thank God, I can stop circling this stupid letter 'o.' " And she angled across the traffic, intending to get into a lane to the right of the two slow-moving, smoke-belching orange behemoths.

"We should have had Vito do this part," Angelo said. "He likes being in one place all the time."

"In jail," Rosa commented.

"I don't think it matters," Angelo said. "Just so it's the same place every minute."

"There he is," Rosa said, cutting off a Peugeot and coming up beside the orange trucks on their right.

Yes, there was Vito, looking even older and wearier and sicker than usual, all bundled and blanketed inside a motorized wheelchair, tentatively and nervously driving his fragile little vehicle right out into all that traffic. He looked terrified, and he'd never been known for his acting ability, so he probably *was* terrified.

"On second thought," Angelo said, as they flashed past Vito, "I'm just as happy to be here and have him out there."

"The Germans," Rosa said, looking in the rearview mirror.

Angelo looked around: "Where?"

"Behind us. Where they're supposed to be."

And so they were; or at least two of them were. The black Volkswagen had fallen into line behind the white Renault, Rudi at the wheel and Herman in the front seat beside him. As for Otto, why, there's Otto over there, the Boche near the Avenue Hoche—Otto was on foot, his chunky torso festooned with cameras, another camera ready in his hands. And Otto was *backing* away from the sidewalk directly into the line of traffic, ignoring all those cars and frowning instead at whatever it was over by Avenue Hoche that he had decided he must at once have permanently recorded on film.

Meanwhile, the driver of the first orange truck, having entered the Place Charles de Gaulle from Avenue Kléber and desiring to continue his northward journey by exiting onto Avenue de Wagram, and seeing Avenue de Wagram nearing him up ahead, attempted to flow across the traffic rightward, thus to leave the busy circling rush of cars; but a little white Renault was in his way. Nestling against the truck's huge right front fender, the Renault seemed as happy with this propinquity as a baby chick under the wing of its mother. The driver of the truck tapped his brakes, intending to ease in behind the white Renault, but all of a sudden a black Volkswagen beetle convertible was also in the way. And the Renault had slowed down, just as a baby chick might when discovering it had rashly leaped out from under its mother's wing.

Avenue de Wagram; it was right *there*. The truck driver braked even more, sounding his horn, edging right as far as he dared, but the Renault and Volkswagen both seemed utterly oblivious of him. No matter how slowly he traveled, both were right there, next to him. He couldn't come to a dead stop, could he?

Too late. Avenue de Wagram was behind him. The goddam Renault and the son-of-a-bitch Volkswagen were still next to him. And he would have to go all the way around the Arc and exit onto Avenue de Wagram on the next circuit.

Hell.

❂

Grinding slowly up the hilly streets of Ménilmontant came a very large, very long truck, its contents covered with a series of silver tarpaulins all tied down with thick ropes. It was a distinctive truck, and Bruddy, looking at it in the rearview mirror of the parked cab, smiled and muttered, "And there you are, right on time." He and Andrew and Sir Mortimer had watched this truck loaded this morning, out at Le Bourget; all the crates and cartons and anonymous packages from the Yerbadoroan plane shifted onto this truck, then covered with the tarpaulins. A little "us drivers together" conversation between Bruddy and the truck's driver had elicited the man's planned route and expected timetable, and the fellow's estimates had been exact; he was where he'd said he would be, at the time he'd guessed.

Bruddy let the big silver truck grind by, struggling its way up the steep hill, then eased the cab into gear and slowly followed.

Meanwhile, much farther up the hill, Andrew stood leaning against the side of a large dirty delivery van, trying to look like a loafing French workman and managing only to look like an English civil servant dressed for gardening. Checking his watch, looking downhill, Andrew sighed and shifted position. Waiting was always the hardest.

Even farther up the hill, Sir Mortimer was purchasing watermelons; half a dozen big juicy ones. He had equipped himself with a baby carriage, sans baby, and while the vegetable peddlar watched in frank bewilderment and curiosity, Sir Mortimer gently placed the six watermelons inside the baby carriage. Noticing the vegetable woman's expression, Sir Mortimer told her, "I am English, Madam, which explains everything. Eccentric, you see."

"Ah!" said the vegetable woman, her brow clearing, a smile of understanding glowing on her face. "L'eccen-*trick!*"

*

Renee, apparently unaware that one too many buttons of her blouse was undone, leaned forward and pointed: "And what is this, with all the lights?"

The three workmen assigned to the freight yard switching office reluctantly diverted their attention from Renee's front to the machine under question: "This tells us," one of the workmen said, smiling at Renee's breasts, "where our locomotives are."

Of those in the switching office, only Jean, over by the window, was at the moment aware that one of their locomotives was in motion down there in the freight yards, with Charles at the controls. Rapidly the locomotive was backing toward the track containing, among others, the two yellow boxcars. Jean surreptitiously moved a lever, while Renee continued to distract the three workmen, and down in the freight yard a switch shifted position just before the locomotive reached it.

*

The driver of the second orange truck had no idea why they just kept going around and around the Arc de Triomphe; was Jacques lost up there? How can you be lost at the Arc de Triomphe? The driver of the second truck tried honking his horn, to attract his compatriot Jacques's attention to the fact that Avenue de Wagram was going by yet again, over there on the right, like an unattainable brass ring at a merry-go-round, but so many other horns were being honked in this area (including the lead truck's, though the second driver couldn't know that) that it had no effect at all.

And there was the girl again. The driver had noticed her the last time around, a very good-looking dark-haired girl on a bicycle, very obviously in terror of her life amid all this traffic. A very good-looking girl. The driver smiled at the sight of her, and followed his friend on around the Arc yet again.

The beautiful Lida, for indeed the girl was she, had drawn the attention of most of the drivers in her general vicinity, but not all of it favorable, since her motion combined the slow and tentative with little spurts and jerks at oblique angles, as though she were riding a bicycle without training wheels for the first time in her life. The effect of Lida on her bicycle, combined with a smiliar effect of Vito nearby in his motorized wheelchair, was not only to fray tempers and risk accidents in an increasingly widening area, but was also to force a slowing of the traffice flow, an unwonted braking and deceleration leading to an increasing back-up of traffic disgorging from the surrounding streets. Add Otto to the mix, obliviously backing into the very heart of the traffic while staring intently into the viewfinder of his camera, and you had all the ingredients for possibly the worst traffic jam in the history of the world.

＊

Checking his watch one last time, Andrew roused himself from his resting position against the large dirty delivery van. Then a bit awkwardly he climbed up and into the van, and with no air of familiarity with the van whatsoever, seated himself behind the wheel. He started the engine, pulled gracelessly out into the traffic, and drove haltingly around the block, coming to a stop facing downhill on a long narrow steep street.

On another street farther uphill, Sir Mortimer strolled with his baby carriage, into which the occasional tourist gazed with an expression that swiftly shifted from expectant pleasure to thorough bewilderment. Sir Mortimer stared down all potential inquiries, and continued slowly on his way, checking his watch.

Farther downhill, the silver-covered truck continued to struggle slowly upward, followed by the London cab containing Bruddy, who alternately tapped his fingers impatiently against the steering wheel and checked his watch.

*

Having shunted the freight cars that had been ahead of the two yellow boxcars onto a nearby track, Charles now manipulated the locomotive through the maze of tracks, watching the switches open and shut along his path, trusting Jean and Renee to be doing their part up in the switching office. Looking up there, Charles could occasionally catch a glimpse of Jean through the large windows, but Renee was out of sight; undoubtedly distracting the employees at the farther end of the room, permitting Jean to get on with the task.

Which was taking too long, but there'd been no help for it; a lot of shifting and shunting had to take place before Charles could even get at those two yellow boxcars.

But now everything else was out of the way, the yellow boxcars were exposed at last, and speedily the little yard locomotive backed along the track—*slide, slide,* went the switches along the way—toward their destination.

*

Were they going to miss Avenue de Wagram *again?* "Jacques!" yelled the driver of the second truck, in useless rage and frustration. "Jacques, Jacques, what's the *matter* with you?" And the driver was just starting to accelerate, determined to come up on Jacques's left and remonstrate with him via the medium of obscene hand gestures, when all at once, directly in his path, a wobbly girl on a bicycle crashed into a doddering old man in a motorized wheelchair. The whole kaboodle collapsed virtually under his wheels, and the shocked driver *stood* on the air brakes, so that the truck, with every wheel locked, did two heavy, loud, bone-jarring bunny hops forward and came to an abrupt stop.

Ignoring the shrieks of horns and squeals of metal scraping metal from behind the truck, and unaware of the white Renault stopping on the right side of his truck just long enough to disgorge a passenger—Angelo—the driver opened his door and leaned out to see if the girl and old man were still both sufficiently alive to be yelled at. They were; in fact, both seemed to have been increased in agility by their mishap, since the motorized wheelchair was suddenly zipping away like a Le Mans racer and the girl on the bicycle had abruptly learned everything about balance and speed, to judge by the manner in which she was hastening away. The driver released the open door in order to shake a fist at the departing miscreants, but all at once he found himself in midair. Someone—Angelo, in fact—had entered his truck cab from the right, and had given him a huge shove.

Truckdrivers were not meant by God to be airborne; at least not for long. This one soon found himself earthbound again, in a discouragingly hard and abrupt manner, and as he rolled over, shocked and disoriented, he discovered that his head was down amid a lot of automobile tires. *Moving* automobile tires.

Oh, no. Up he jumped, and looked around, and his truck was going away!

"Hi! Hi!"

The former driver of the departing truck started to run after his machine, and was promptly nearly run down by a black Volkswagen beetle convertible. Then the damn Volkswagen continued to be in his way, because the driver insisted on stopping and making no-doubt-disparaging remarks to the former-truckdriver-now-pedestrian in German. The last straw; German.

And his truck was gone.

*

Checking his watch, Andrew put the delivery van in neutral, released the emergency brake, and stepped out to the steep cobbled street. Slowly, then more quickly, the delivery van rolled away alone down the street.

Checking his watch, Sir Mortimer walked around the corner, gave the baby carriage a slight shove, and stood observing the carriage's trajectory as it bounced and trundled down the long steep hill.

Checking his watch, Bruddy accelerated the cab, angled out, rapidly passed the still-climbing silver-garbed truck, and then braked to a stop at the curb half a block farther up the hill; not far from an intersection. (A dirty white delivery van could be seen coming downhill, this way.) Bruddy climbed out of the cab and watched the silver truck slowly approach.

*

"Why, no," Renee said, her smile glazing a bit, "the coffee isn't too strong at all." She sat on a desk, swinging her crossed leg, smiling and smiling and smiling.

Across the room, Jean watched out the large plate glass

windows as a small yard locomotive trundled away out of the yards, bearing behind it two gleaming yellow boxcars.

The smile on Jean's face was much more realistic than the smile on the face of Renee.

*

Unaware of the awful twist of fate that had befallen his friend and co-worker behind him, Jacques, the driver of the first orange truck, continued his frustrating, enraging but unstoppable circling of the Arc de Triomphe until, just about opposite the place where his cohort had come a cropper, Jacques too was forced to suddenly stand on his air brakes; too late. The stout German tourist looking so intently into his viewfinder gave out a sudden hoarse cry of despair, threw up his arms, and in a flurry of cameras he dropped beneath the wheels of the truck.

"Sacre!" cried the driver. "Merde!" And he leaped from the truck to run to the tourist, who sprawled moaning on the pavement next to the huge left front tire of the vehicle which had apparently written finis to his career in amateur photography. "Are you dead?" cried the driver. "Do you yet live?"

"*Aaaaiiiiiiiiiyyyyyyyyyeeeeeeeeeee,*" said Otto.

The driver sank to one knee beside his victim. "My poor friend," he said. "I fear you have given your life for your art."

Otto reached upward, feebly clutched at the driver's lapels. "Oooooooooooh," said Otto, tugging at the driver's lapels.

"You want to tell me something?" The driver leaned close to Otto's mouth. "Yes? Yes?"

Just behind the driver now was the big left front

wheel of his truck and now, as he listened very carefully to Otto gulp and swallow and gasp, that big left front wheel began to turn. It moved, it rolled, it went away, shortly to be followed by the left rear wheel of the truck cab.

"Glug," said Otto. "Gll gll. Glug."

"Yes?" the driver asked. "Do you want me to notify someone?" The driver made as though to look around for help, but Otto gave a sudden spastic tug on his lapels, and gulped ever more dramatically and impressively.

The left front wheel of the truck trailer went by.

The left rear wheel of the truck trailer went by.

"Yes?" The driver, though remorseful, was also becoming impatient. "You wish to say something? Say it, please, *say* it!"

"Help me up," said Otto, in a clear and distinct voice.

"Are you sure you should be moved?"

"Oh, yes," Otto said. "Absolutely. Help me up."

A frown of bewilderment creased the driver's face. He reared back, the better to look at Otto, but Otto continued to clutch his lapels and therefore came along with him. The driver went on rearing back, trying to get away from this suddenly-healthy-looking face, and in that manner both the driver and Otto came erect, at which point Otto released the driver's lapels and said, "Thank you very much."

The driver gaped. "Aren't you—?"

"I feel much better now," Otto said, and turned away, and reached out his hand. Providentially, it would seem, a black Volkswagen beetle convertible screeched to a halt right next to them, in such a manner that the VW's door-handle nestled in Otto's waiting fingers. Otto opened the car door, entered the VW, and was driven away.

The truckdriver stared. Horns honked all around him, to indicate that he was standing in the middle of impatient traffic. Shaking his head, he turned around, reached out his own hand for the handle of his truck door, and stopped, frozen, staring.

His truck was gone.

❖

The driver of the silver-garbed truck struggling northward up the hills of Ménilmontant tapped his brakes when he saw the dirty white delivery van bouncing down the street toward him, veering left and right on the uneven cobblestone street. "He'll cause an accident, that one," the driver muttered to himself, and then watched with horror as a baby carriage, alone and unattended, all at once appeared from the side street, rolling out directly into the path of the oncoming delivery van.

Which didn't stop. Which didn't even slow down. "Look *out!*" the driver of the silver-garbed truck screamed, and released his wheel to clutch at his temples as the delivery van *crashed* into the baby carriage, reducing it to a model of the Beaubourg Museum. Several pieces of something flew up and out of the baby carriage, red and juicy, and splatted onto the cobblestones.

"MY GOD!" cried the driver of the silver-garbed truck. Slamming on his hand brake, he jumped out of the truck and ran forward, staring at the horror spread across the street.

The delivery van, its path altered by the accident, had bumped up over the tall curb and come to a stop against a shop window, which was still shimmering from the impact but which had not quite broken. The baby carriage, its agony over, lay twisted in the middle of the street. And the red juicy stuff?

The driver went down on one knee. He picked something up and stared at it. Meanwhile, shopkeepers and pedestrians and coffee-drinkers and aperitif-drinkers of the arrondissement were running forward, clustering around, staring and clucking and looking sick to their stomachs.

The driver was reduced to stuttering. "Passe-passe," he said, displaying the red sticky juicy stuff to revolted on-lookers; but "passe-passe" means conjuring, magic, sorcery, which was surely not what he meant. Onward: "Passe-temps," he stuttered next, which had to be another error, as "passe-temps" means in English pastime, game, foolery. And at last the driver got it out: "Pastèque!" he cried, and to all those who thought he was still babbling, still stuttering, we put the lie, because he was absolutely correct, because in English the word "pastèque" is—

"Watermelon!"

"Honk!" said a vehicle, and the driver with his hands full of watermelon moved to one side, and a truck labored on past him and up the hill. A large heavy truck, its cargo sheathed with silver tarpaulins, and its wheel manned—though the driver couldn't know this—by Bruddy Dunk.

"My truck!" The driver pointed watermelon. "They have my truck!" And he ran forward, only to have his way blocked by the sudden appearance across his path of a black London taxicab.

A London taxicab? In Paris? What foolishness! "Out of my way!" cried the driver. "They have taken my truck!"

The passenger of the London taxicab, who happened to be Andrew Pinkenham himself, lowered his window and spoke in oblivious unconcern (and in English), asking the truckdriver, "I do beg your pardon, but can you direct my driver to Calais?"

The truckdriver didn't speak English even when life was being calm; at a moment like this, he barely spoke French. "My truck!" he yelled, pointing watermelon over the taxi roof at the vehicle in question, which was now just cresting the top of the hill and disappearing down the long straight rapid slope of the other side.

"No," Andrew said, unruffled and unheeding. "Calais. I'm afraid my driver is lost."

Whereas the truckdriver was going berserk: "My truck! My truck! Out of the way!" And he kicked ferociously at the side of the taxi.

"I don't believe he knows," Andrew said, and leaned forward, calling to Sir Mortimer at the cab wheel, "Drive on."

"Right, guv," Sir Mortimer said, in a terrible attempt at a Cockney accent (but what do the French know about Cockney accents anyway?), and the London taxicab rolled serenely away.

And the former driver of the silver-garbed truck, completely out of his mind, stood throwing pieces of watermelon at people in the middle of the street until the gendarmes came and sympathetically hit him on the head a lot with their sticks and carried him away.

10

Eustace was going crazy. Everything was organized, everything was in motion, but was everything going the way it was supposed to go?

What Eustace wanted, what Eustace needed, was for the entire city of Paris to suddenly be magically reduced to the size and aspect of a model train layout, with himself on a high stool overlooking the whole thing. Then he could *see* if the English contingent was doing its job in Ménilmontant, he could *see* if the French contingent was succesfully performing its task in the Gare de la Chappelle, he could *see* if the Italians and the Germans were performing profitably at the Arc de Triomphe. Instead of which, here he was on this windy hotel roof, seated in this wobbly folding chair at this rickety folding table, holding down all his maps and charts and memorandums with these *god damn* walkietalkies, and trying to get somebody somewhere to tell him *what in hell is going on.*

Eustace picked up a walkie-talkie at random, then slapped his palm down on the two maps and the diagram before they could blow away. Into the walkie-talkie he said,

"Group—" then hesitated, frowned, turned the walkie-talkie over, and read the white letter painted there: "—C. Group C, come in. Come in, Group C." Then he held the walkie-talkie close to his ear, and listened to several people laughing in French: "Rire, rire, rire, rire, rire," they were saying.

"Oh, really," Eustace said, slapped the walkie-talkie down, yanked up another, grabbed for the memos too late, watched them blow off the roof, swore in English, read the letter on the walkie-talkie, and yelled into it, "Group D! Say something, Group D!"

Shrill voices gabbled in Italian.

"Stop it," Eustace said, very sternly, into the walkie-talkie. "Now, just stop all that. I'm serious about this. This is a serious business."

Gabble-gabble-gabble.

Gabble. A different gabble, different in tone, different in language, and different in place. A live gabble, in fact. Baffled, Eustace turned his head and saw Lida's cousin standing there, looking as stubborn as—and less intelligent than—a mule. "Not you again," Eustace said.

In Spanish, Manuel repeated his gabble, which was simply, "What have you done with Lida?"

"I don't have time for this now," Eustace told him. "I have all these other idiots to contend with."

"I demand to see Lida," insisted Manuel.

Eustace chose another walkie-talkie, spoke firmly into it: "Group A, I wish a report, and I wish no nonsense, no foreign tongues, no conclave-of-nations, nothing but a *progress report* concerning the *progress* of our *present operation!*"

"In München steht ein Hofbräuhaus," sang the walkie-talkie, into badly assorted voices, "eins, zwei, *gsuffa!*"

Manuel had plodded around in front of Eustace, and

was standing just the other side of the table. Ignoring the singing walkie-talkie, he said, "You tell me where Lida is."

Bewildered, appalled, Eustace was asking the walkie-talkie, "Are you all drunk?"

Manuel pounded the table; all the walkie-talkies hopped. "Tell me where Lida is!"

Eustace glared at him. "Can't you see I'm busy?"

"I don't trust you people. I want Lida. Lida! Lida!"

Eustace picked the familiar name out of the gabble. "Oh, Lida, is it? Your cousin, eh, that's what you want?"

"Lida," agreed Manuel, sullen and implacable.

Eustace waved an airy hand—made somewhat less airy by the fact that it was still grasping a walkie-talkie—out over the city: "Lida," he said, "is out peddling her bicycle around Paris. Go away now."

"Lida," said Manuel.

Eustace reared up from his folding chair, shaking the walkie-talkie under Manuel's chin, yelling at him, "You go away! You're one idiot too many, one language too many! I don't have the time or the patience for you! Go away, or I'll, I'll—" Eustace gabbled a bit himself, waving both arms. "I'll throw you off this roof!"

Manuel might not speak any language but Spanish—and a rather bedraggled form of South American Spanish at that—but he could read faces and tones of voice pretty well, and he was smart enough to back away from Eustace and those waving arms, saying as he did so, "You'll regret this. You'll be sorry about this!"

Go!" screamed Eustace. "Go go go go go!"

Manuel went, muttering in Spanish. Eustace flung down the still-singing-in-German walkie-talkie, grabbed up another one, and yelled into it, "Somebody say something in English!"

And the voice of Bruddy, angry and belligerent, came immediately back, saying, "What do you bloody well expect, Hindustani?"

"Thank God," Eustace said. "A friendly voice. Where are you?"

Bruddy's voice said, "In the flippin truck, you twit. Where are you?"

"Where am I?" Baffled at such a question, Eustace looked around before answering, "I'm on the roof."

"Good place for a pigeon like you."

Belatedly, Eustace realized what Bruddy had said earlier, and he cried out, "In the *truck?* You mean, you've *done* it?"

"Bloody twit," responded Bruddy.

Before Eustace could continue this suddenly invigorating conversation, one of the other walkie-talkies on the table suddenly said, in Jean LeFraque's Gallic-accented English, "Hello. This is me. Is that you?"

"Wait, Br— Uhh, Group—" (quick reading of painted letter) "—B. Don't go way, just wait." And Eustace dropped that walkie-talkie, picked up another one and said, "Is that you, Group C?"

The walkie-talkie squabbled, in Italian.

"Arrgh!" Eustace flung it down, looked at the others, found the one with the "C" painted on it, picked it up, and cried into it, "Group C? Is that you?"

"I don't know," answered Jean. "Am I Group C?"

"Yes, of course you are."

"I can never remember."

"You wanted something?" In his desperation, Eustace was squeezing the walkie-talkie with both hands. "Is something wrong? What's gone wrong?"

"Mission accomplished," said the happy voice of Jean LeFraque.

Too prepared by now for calamity, Eustace failed at first to take in the import of Jean's message. "What?" he said. "Isn't it work— *What?* You've done it?"

"Absolutely. That's how you say it? Absolute*ly?*"

"Absolutely!" responded Eustace, a huge smile crossing his face. "Absolute-*ment!*"

"What a charming accent you have," Jean said drily, but Eustace had already dropped that walkie-talkie and was lunging for another, shouting into it, "Br— B. Group B. You're in the truck?"

"Same as ever," came Bruddy's surly voice.

"It's working!" Eustace cried. He jumped to his feet, grabbing up the walkie-talkies into his arms and dancing with them. Gusts of wind flipped and flew his maps, his charts, his diagrams; Eustace in his dancing kicked over his folding chair. Somewhere in the distance a red balloon rose up into the blue Parisian sky. The walkie-talkies sang and snarled and squabbled at one another, and Eustace danced on the roof.

11

The construction business is booming in Paris, and has been for the past several years. Office buildings, apartment houses, they're shooting up everywhere, within the city limits and just beyond, steel and concrete and glass creating cell after cell as Paris expands and expands, ever upward.

But in times of boom there are always those who boom a little too enthusiastically, who overextend their capacities, their finances, their resources, and who suddenly find themselves in bankruptcy court, surrounded by no-longer-smiling faces. People are never understanding in such situations, just never understanding.

And when such mishaps occur, unfinished buildings inevitably molder, roofless, wall-less, worker-less, hopeless, awaiting a new owner, a new builder, a new infusion of hope and vision and capital.

Just such a structure was the incomplete apartment house on the Boulevard Berthier in the 17th Arrondissement, in the northwest corner of the city. Behind a tall rickety wooden fence languished the pale white concrete skeleton of what might still someday be a finished building but which at the moment looked most like a cubist version of a museum's dinosaur skeleton. The white concrete walls, with their gaping rectangular holes, jutted up from yellowish mud, giving every evidence of failure and despair. Who would come to such a place, unless forced to by circumstance?

Rosa Palermo, that's who. And Angelo Salvagambelli. And Vito Palone. Angelo having driven orange truck number two through the wooden gate in the wooden fence, followed by Rosa and Vito in the little white Renault, Vito had reclosed the wooden gate and now the Italian mob was considering the results of its depredation. They were, in point of fact, getting down to cases.

Shipping cases. Great huge wooden shipping cases now lay jumbled beside the orange truck, and here came Angelo and Vito staggering out of the back of the truck with yet another. They dropped it off the rear of the truck, hopped down into the mud next to it, and paused to lean against the case and mop their brows with their sleeves.

"Well," Angelo said. "Nearly empty. We'll put this one over there."

"No," said Vito. "I must rest."

Dubious, Angelo looked around, saying, "I suppose we could open some of these now, and unload the rest later."

"Opening crates," Vito told him, "is not the same as resting."

Angelo frowned at him. "Don't you want seven billion lire?"

"Give me an advance on it now," Vito suggested, "and I'll go *hire* someone to open the crates."

"Vito," Angelo said, his manner at the same time patronizing yet truly sympathetic, "what's the matter with you?"

"I'm an old man," Vito pointed out. "Until you and that

105

virago came along, I was retired. They never made me work like this in prison."

"Seven billion lire," Angelo repeated. "You could buy a yacht, and sail the Adriatic."

"It's polluted," said Vito.

"Sail the Aegean," Angelo offered.

"It's polluted."

"Then sail the Mediterranean!"

"It's polluted."

Angelo raised his eyes to heaven. "Then," he said, "sail the Atlantic Ocean!"

Vito shrugged. "It's polluted," he said.

"Then don't sail at all," Angelo told him. Angelo had become very angry, mostly because he had no idea how he'd gotten into this conversation in the first place. "Do I care if you sail? Does it matter to me if you sail or not? *Don't* sail!"

Infuriatingly calm, Vito said, "I'll sail if I want to sail."

Angelo, hands clenched into fists, was still formulating his answer when Rosa came striding around the corner of the unfinished building, glaring at them both and saying, "What's with you two? What are you doing?"

"I'm resting my heart," Vito told her.

"I'm working?" Rosa demanded. "I'm standing guard out by the road? And you two loaf?"

"I'll trade places with you," Vito suggested.

"To do what?"

"To unload the truck."

Rosa couldn't believe it. "You," she demanded, "would ask a *woman* to do such a job? A woman like your own mother?"

"All right," Vito said. "All right."

"A woman like your sisters," Rosa said.

Vito, defeated, climbed back up into the truck, saying, "Yes, yes, I'm going."

Angelo, cheerful, vaulted up into the truck: "Here we go, then," he said.

Rosa stepped forward to yell into the truck: "A woman like the Holy Virgin!"

"All *right*," Vito's voice came, plaintively, from within the truck. "All right all right all right. I didn't mean it."

✴

Even Paris has junkyards, and even junkyards can prove unprofitable business ventures. In such a junkyard, containing dead auto parts but no fat men in undershirts and not even one killer dog, Andrew Pinkenham and Sir Mortimer Maxwell sat in the sunlight on a pair of ripped and tattered automobile seats, and continued their earlier discussion, while at some remove Bruddy Dunk completed the task of removing all the tarpaulins from their recently acquired truck.

"Look at it this way, Sir Mortimer," Andrew was saying. "If we don't take it all, how can they be sure of anything? We take half for ourselves, and give them the other half, and nobody the wiser."

"I'm opposed to it," Sir Mortimer insisted. "It's too dangerous."

"But it isn't dangerous at all," Andrew assured him. "No one knows precisely how valuable this haul is supposed to be; if the result is less than the expectation, it won't be the first time in the history of the world."

Bruddy approached from the truck as Sir Mortimer shook his head, saying, "It won't work."

"Neither will I," Bruddy informed them, "if you two don't hop to it. I'm not the only haul-and-tugger present."

"Absolutely right, Bruddy," Andrew said, getting briskly to his feet. "Here we come."

"This discussion," Sir Mortimer said, obstinately, as more slowly and reluctantly he too stood up, "remains open."

❋

Progress doesn't merely add; it also subtracts. One of the unfortunate subtractions currently under way in Paris is the gradual filling in and removal of the system of canals running northward through the eastern part of the city from the Seine to the suburb of Pantin and beyond. At one time, goods from northeastern France and meat from the slaughterhouses of the 19th Arrondissement were barged south along the Canal St. Denis and the Canal de l'Ourcq into the Bassin de la Villette, just north of the Place de Stalingrad. From there, the waterway tunneled beneath Place de Stalingrad and underwent a change of name, becoming the Canal St. Martin as it zigzagged southward through the 10th Arrondissement. Running through the 11th Arrondissement, the canal has been covered by the Boulevard Richard Lenoir, but the waterway still exists, in slimy and rat-infested darkness, beneath the broad boulevard, and at last re-emerges just south of the Place de la Bastille, where this last section just north of the Seine is called the Gare de l'Arsenal, and is the only segment of the canal still in any kind of ordinary use.

The rest of the canal is dying, and nearly dead. Plans are afoot not merely to cover the canal over, as in the Boulevard Richard Lenoir section, but actually to fill it in, to stop the flow of water forever. And from a practical standpoint the canal, while remaining rather attractive here and there, has ceased to be useful. The locks don't work, the roofs make barge traffic impossible, and only the smallest rowboats can negotiate the canal at all. For many practical reasons, the canal shall die. Too bad it never became a tourist attraction.

The death of the canal has decreed a kind of slow death to many of the buildings which once served it as warehouses and offices, storage areas for the goods shipped along the waterway. Particularly in the northeast corner of the city, up around Boulevard Macdonald, the big hulking empty warehouses remain, their stone walls lapped by the dirty idle useless water of the canal.

It was in one such abandoned warehouse that Herman Muller and Otto Berg and Rudi Schlisselmann briskly unloaded the truck they'd so recently acquired at the Arc de Triomphe. Much of the contents of this truck was building blocks, large blocks of shaped gray stone, very heavy and authentic-looking, and it was while carrying one of these that Otto suddenly said, "Look at this. These blocks are all numbered."

"Naturally," Herman told him. "That's so the building can be properly reassembled."

"This one," Otto said, squinting to read the painted-on numbers, "is L-274."

Rudi, just emerging from the truck with another block, said, "Mine's L-273."

"They must go together," Otto suggested.

While Herman went back into the truck, Otto and Rudi put their blocks down side by side. Looking around, Otto said, "I wonder where L-275 is."

Rudi started poking through the blocks they'd already removed from the truck: "Most of these have different first letters. Here're some R's, here're a couple F's. . . ."

Emerging from the truck, Herman said, "L-275? I've got it here."

Taking it from him, Otto said, "Good, good." He placed it in its proper position with the first two.

Rudi, still poking among the other blocks, said, "Here's L-267."

"Not yet," Otto told him. "Put it to one side."

❋

Subway systems both expand and contract. New York, London, all the older systems have no-longer-used stations, even no-longer-used sublines. Paris is no exception, with several abandoned Métro stops; such as the one under the intersection of Rue du Four and Rue du Cherche-Midi, for instance, on the Left Bank, not far from the center of artistic Paris, the corner of Boulevard St. Germain and Boul' Mich'. This unused stop is on Line Number 10, the one between Porte d'Auteuil and the Gare d'Orléans/Austerlitz. The stop is in fact between the still-used stops of Sèvres-Babylone and Mabillon, and may be seen from your Métro window; look closely.

At such an abandoned station, on an equally abandoned spur line, now stood the two yellow boxcars from the freight yards behind the Gare de la Chappelle, along with the little switching locomotive which had removed them from the ken of the railroad. The boxcar doors were open, and Charles Moule and Jean LeFraque were carrying out from them an endless array of sofas, chairs, lamps, tables, beds, and other furniture and furnishings. Renee Chateaupierre stood to one side, thoughtfully considering the platform, on which a room was gradually being assembled, under her instructions:

"Put that there. Yes, that's right, put it right there. And that lamp over there. No, wait; I think it would be better over there, next to the love seat. No, don't put that there, it clashes with the sofa. Let me see now, it should go, hmmm . . ."

"Decide, will you?" Charles asked, plaintively, the cigarette bobbing in the corner of his mouth. "This is heavy."

"I'm doing my best," Renee told him. "There, I think. Put it there. We can always move it later, if it offends."

12

The atmosphere in the Robespierre Suite of the Hotel Vendôme was gloomy in the extreme, plus lightning flashes. His Excellency Escobar Lynch, El Presidente of Yerbadoro, paced the Persian carpet with the grim and purposeful tread of the Grim Reaper himself, while his wife Maria moved about the room in short violent bursts of unfocused energy, like a catamaran on a gusty sea. The police detective who had drawn the short straw back at Headquarters, and was as a result the one to interview El Presidente Lynch and his First Lady on the subject of the theft, serially, of their castle from various points around Paris, had the pained expression of an agnostic in a lion's den, and the two uniformed police officers who had come here with him were remaining firmly and silently in the background, pretending to be floor lamps.

The common language between the detective and the Lynches was neither French nor Spanish but English, in which El Presidente was fluent, Maria was voluble, and the detective was extremely Gallic. As when, in an accent as soft and twisty as a croissant, he said, "We are making progress, Mr. President."

"I had a castle," Escobar Lynch pointed out, "and now I do not have a castle. I fail to see where that could be termed progress."

"We have made several arrests," the detective said. "Our police are scouring the slums."

Dangerously quiet, like a distant thunderstorm, Escobar said, "You expect to find my castle in the slums?"

Maria paused in her spurting and tacking hither and yon about the room to wave her arms over her head and cry, "Why doesn't somebody *do* something?"

"We are making progress, Madam," the detective promised her, with a tiny apologetic smile that begged for mercy.

Maria had no mercy: "You must be *quick*," she said, tacking toward the detective, pointing a long-nailed, sharp-nailed, ruby-nailed finger at his nose. "You're much too *slow*."

The detective blinked and swallowed. "We have already made several arrests," he said.

"You said that before," Escobar pointed out.

"It remains true," the detective said. "A castle is not that easy to hide. Surely before long we—"

Escobar said, "Before long is not good enough. By then, they may have . . . stolen things from it. Valuable paintings, perhaps, or, uh, things of sentimental value."

It was not the detective's job to wonder what things of sentimental value the Lynches might possibly possess. It was his job to soothe the Lynches, to the degree that such soothing could be effected, and to hope that his confreres in the field actually were making progress on the discovery and return of Escondido Castle. "We have the bills of lading," he assured Escobar. "The castle and its contents are fully itemized. When we find it—"

"Yes," Maria said, swooping close. "When you find it.

That's the question, that's it in a nutshell. When *will* you find it?"

"We are making progress," the detective stammered, thoroughly rattled by Maria's swooping manner. "We have already made several arrests."

The dryness of his tone suggesting he might become murderous at any instant, Escobar said, "And you are scouring the slums."

"Er, yes."

Turning on Escobar, Maria said, "If this man remains in our room much longer, I believe I shall bite him on the neck. Very hard."

The detective blanched, and raised a protective hand shakily to his neck.

His manner almost kindly, Escobar told the detective, "Perhaps you had best return to your duties."

"We will report all developments," the detective promised.

'Grrr," said Maria.

"By telephone," the detective said, and fled.

13

Through the piles of fenders, heaps of bumpers, mounds of hubcaps, monkey bars of axles, doughnut trays of tires, through the whole rusting, glinting, metal crazy quilt of the abandoned junkyard, Eustace Dench, successful (yet again) master criminal, steered his poot-pooting motorcycle, with Lida Perez the beautiful revolutionary in the sidecar. Around a final fortress of hoods Eustace steered the machine, and stopped in a small clearing where Bruddy and Andrew and Sir Mortimer labored away at the unpacking of many many crates. All three looked up at the sound of the motorcycle's roar, then went back to work again when they saw who it was.

Eustace switched off the motor and jumped off the cycle; Lida remained in the sidecar, looking valiant but short. Approaching his unpacking countrymen, Eustace said, "Well, well, well, and how's it coming along?"

Removing from a crate a hideous red-and-gold table lamp with a fringed shade and a woodland scene on the base featuring nymphs and shepherds in fairly graphic contact, and holding this object aloft, Sir Mortimer said, "These people have execrable taste."

"It isn't their taste we care about," Eustace pointed out. "It's their income."

"Well put," Andrew said, carefully placing to one side a ceramic cigarette box whose handle was a pair of fornicating goats.

"None of this income come through here yet," Bruddy said.

"Well, keep on with it," Eustace said. "I have the walkie-talkies in the sidecar; give me a tinkle if you find anything."

"I have the walkie-talkies in the sidecar," echoed Sir Mortimer, his mouth curling like a rabid dog's. "That such a sentence is even *possible* in the English language almost makes me lose hope."

Andrew said, "Don't forget the tinkle."

"We'll be off, then," Eustace said, hopped on his motorcycle, gave them all a cheery wave, started the engine, and roared away.

●

When Eustace and Lida and the motorcycle and the sidecar arrived at the site of the incomplete apartment building, they found the Italian contingent completely surrounded by plumbing. Tubs, sinks, bidets, urinals, medicine cabinets, shower stalls, all were scattered here and there in the mud, sprinkled with excelsior and garnished with shredded wood. Ignoring the mutinous expressions on the faces of Rosa and Angelo and Vito, Eustace gaily hopped off his machine once more and strode through the mud, calling, "And how are we all doing, eh? Eh?"

"You see what we have here," Vito said, in Italian, gesturing with his horny hand at all the porcelain in sight.

"Seven billion lire," Angelo said, in tones of deepest

sarcasm and disgust. "What we have is seven billion bathrooms."

"Now, don't you boys start talking Italian at me," Eustace said, with a smile and a playful waggle of his finger; he was in too good a mood from the success of the operation to be seriously bothered by these continuing linguistic problems. Turning to Rosa, he said, "No luck yet, eh?"

But Vito wasn't done speaking Italian: "I was dragged out of retirement for this," he said. "To become a stevedore in my old age."

Nor was Angelo: "And to be driven on," he said bitterly, "like a mule, by a harridan of a woman."

"So that's the way you talk about me, is it?" Rosa demanded, flaring at him, hands on hips. "And in front of foreigners too?"

"He doesn't understand," Angelo said. "He doesn't understand anything."

"Well, *I* understand," Rosa told him, "and I—"

"Rosa, Rosa," Eustace said. "Please, Rosa, speak to me and speak in English. I take it you've had no luck yet."

"Luck?" Rosa echoed. "Oh, we've had luck. Wonderful luck. We have enough bathrooms here for a Hilton hotel. *That's* the kind of luck we have."

Eustace peered into the back of the truck, saying, "You still have a chance. It's almost half full."

Gesturing disdainfully at Angelo and Vito, Rosa said, "*These* weaklings had to stop for a nap." Then, turning to the men under consideration and switching to Italian, she yelled, "A *nap* you had to stop for!"

"If I ever get back to Italy," Angelo told her, "I will hire a women to kill you."

"Oh, yes, you're full of talk," Rosa said. "All you do is talk."

Coming close to Eustace, looking him in the eye and opening his mouth to show his old, stained, cracked, broken teeth, Vito said, "*You* led us on this Children's Crusade, Englishman. Are you pleased with yourself?"

Smiling amiably in the teeth of those teeth, Eustace said, "Yes, we're all doing our best. But I have to go now." And he retreated from those teeth, hopping once again onto his motorcycle, giving Lida a bright and meaningless smile.

"Perhaps," Angelo said with grim cheerfulness to Rosa, "this lunatic will run you down with his motorcycle."

"Yes, you're doing just fine," Eustace told Angelo. He waved, he started the motor, and he cycled away.

❖

One end of the platform of the unused Métro station had become a kind of stage set, a sort of living room without walls, completely—perhaps overly—furnished with sofas, chairs, lamps, carpets, tables, and so on. A few of the lamps were even lit, increasing the effect, and the final touch was the beautiful Renee, seated on a sofa with a lit lamp beside her, feet curled under her lovely bottom as she leafed through a copy of *Elle*.

Eustace and Lida entered, stage left, looking around in disbelief. Renee, the proper hostess, got to her feet to welcome them, tossing the magazine onto a coffee table. "Ah," she said. "Our first guests. Come in and sit down."

Eustace didn't need to understand French to comprehend the gist of what she'd said. "Incredible," he responded, shaking his head. Then he said, "Where's Jean?" He repeated the name three more times, with three different approximations of a French accent. "Jean. Jean. Jean. Where - is - he?"

With a careless wave toward the far end of the platform, Renee said, "The men are at work."

"I'll be right back," Eustace told Lida, and exited, stage right.

Renee smiled at Lida, saying, "You don't speak French, do you?"

Smiling back, replying in Spanish, Lida said, "I'm sorry, I don't speak French. I speak Spanish and English."

"But it doesn't matter, between women," Renee said.

"But it shouldn't matter, between us," Lida said. "We are both women."

Renee gestured at a comfortable-looking chair. "Do sit down. You know how men are, they'll be talking back there forever."

Back there, by the yellow boxcars and the locomotive, was a completely different world, the transmogrification here being from subway platform to warehouse. Crates and building blocks and odd pieces of furniture were stacked everywhere, with Jean and Charles hard at work with crowbars, opening the wooden crates and emptying out their contents.

As they worked, the two men discussed potential futures. "Of course," Charles said, "if we do find the money, and if we take it away ourselves, we won't be able to stay in France."

"Oh, no, I disagree," Jean told him. "The others would know right away that we'd taken it if we were to leave the country."

Charles said, "But what's the good of cheating the others if we can't spend it? I'll go to the Caribbean, one of the French islands there, and open a bar."

"They'll follow you," Jean told him. "All of them."

"They wouldn't find me. Never in a million years."

119

"Hst," Jean said. "Here comes Eustace."

"He doesn't understand French," Charles pointed out.

"He understands the doublecross," Jean told him, "in any language. Caution, my friend." And turning to the approaching Eustace, he said, "Hello, my friend. How goes it?"

"Just fine," Eustace told him, and spread his smile to include Charles. "How goes it with you two?"

"As you see." Jean gestured around at the goods piled up on the platform. "Some things of value, here and there, but not the major reward we've been promised."

"We'll find it," Eustace said cheerfully. "No doubt at all. Keep me informed, my friend."

"But of course, my friend."

The two friends smiled upon one another.

＊

Eustace knocked sharply on the large wooden door of the abandoned warehouse beside the Canal St. Denis, and was rewarded by the door squeakily rolling open to reveal the round face of Otto, who looked at Eustace and Lida with impatience and said, in German, "Come in, come in. Quick. And don't make so much noise."

"Ah, Otto," Eustace said, stepping into the warehouse. "Where's Herman? I take it you haven't found—" And he stopped, staring across the large empty floor. "Good God," he said.

There, on the other side of the empty space, stood a castle; or that is, a castle segment. It was like something seen in some wayward corner of Disneyland, a castle wing all self-contained, unattached from reality, constructed of stone blocks, with a large wooden door and a couple of windows. Standing in front of this Gothic fantasy, looking stern and efficient, was Herman.

Eustace approached him, gesturing vaguely at the castle-manqué, saying, "Herman? What *is* this?"

"We have nothing to report as yet," Herman told him.

"But—" Eustace moved closer to the castle, peering at it. "But what are you *doing?*" You're supposed to search the castle, not live in it!"

The castle door opened and Rudi came out. He frowned at Eustace, then turned to Herman, saying, "What's the matter with that one now?"

"He doesn't like our construction," Herman told him.

"Oh, no? I'd like to see him do it better."

Switching back to English, Herman told Eustace, "You can rest assured we have examined each and every element before putting it in its place. Neat work habits produce better results."

Eustace dithered, unable to express any of what he was feeling. "But—but—"

"As I told you," Herman went inexorably on, "we have as yet nothing to report. Excuse me, we have a schedule to maintain."

"I—"

"Unless you had something of importance?"

"No, I—"

"Very well, then," Herman said, and joined Otto and Rudi, who were carefully putting more castle pieces together.

Eustace watched open-mouthed for a few seconds, then shook his head as though to gather his wits, spread his hands, shrugged, and said, "Well, if that's the method you prefer, I suppose, um, well . . . Do get in touch if you come up with something."

"Of course," Herman said.

Eustace seemed to want to say something more, but no more came out. After a few more seconds of indecision, he simply turned about and walked away, followed by Lida, going out of the warehouse and closing the door.

"I don't see what he's complaining about," Rudi said, fitting a block into place. "We have the angles right and everything."

"The English just complain," Otto said, picking up another block. "It doesn't mean anything, they just do it all the time. It's the weather they grow up with, it—"

Otto turned the block, looking for its identifying number, and the block tinkled. A clinking sound, like coins falling. Or a gold necklace, perhaps.

Rudi and Herman both froze. They turned their heads. They looked at Otto, who blinked and looked back and turned the block again.

Clink-*chunk*.

"Ah," said Herman. "Ah. Ah. Ah."

14

The Parc des Buttes-Chaumont, in the 19th Arrondissement, in the northeast quarter of Paris, is high and hilly and very untamed, with long wandering paths surrounded by thick shrubbery and proud tall ancient trees. Having driven his motorcycle to the top of one of the hills in this park, Eustace could if he wished look west toward the hills of Ménilmontant, or south toward the Seine, or even north toward the warehouse where Otto and Rudi and Herman were shaking blocks of stone at one another like castanets; but sightseeing was not his purpose here. Communication was his purpose. From this vantage point, the walkie-talkies gave the clearest and strongest signal, and from now on until the search was completed Eustace intended to use this hilltop as his command post.

"Well, now," Eustace said to Lida, after he had switched off the engine, "just start handing me those walkie-talkies, my dear."

"Yes, of course." The walkie-talkies were inside the sidecar, down by her feet. She pulled one out and handed it to Eustace, who read the letter painted on it, pushed the button, and said:

"Hello, Group D."

Nothing. Eustace shook his head with annoyance; could they never get themselves organized on the communication front? "Hello, Group D," he repeated. "Are you there?"

And Rosa's enraged voice snarled from the walkie-talkie, "Yes, I'm here! Where do you suppose I'd be?"

Unruffled, Eustace said, "Nothing yet?"

"We found a kitchen sink," said Rosa's savage voice. "Go drown yourself, Eustace."

Handing the walkie-talkie back to Lida, Eustace told her, "Nothing there yet. Next, please." She handed him another and he spoke into it, "Hello, Group B?"

And it was this time the cheerful voice of Andrew that came back, saying, "Yes, hello, how are you?"

"I'm fine," Eustace told him.

"And so am I," Andrew said. "By God, but this weather is magnificent. I may retire in France yet."

"Yes, well," Eustace said, "that's all very nice. But have you found anything yet to retire *with?*"

"What?" Andrew asked, then said, "Oh. The goods, you mean."

"Right."

"Not a glimmer; sorry, old man. But we're still soldiering on."

"That's fine," Eustace said. "Over and out."

Eustace was about to hand the walkie-talkie to Lida, but Andrew's voice came from it again, saying, "I beg your pardon?"

Eustace pushed the button: "I said over and out. That means I'm hanging up now."

Andrew said, "Does it really?"

"I believe so, yes."

"Fancy. Well, ta."

"Ta," Eustace agreed, and this time he and Lida did

exchange walkie-talkies again, and he said into the new one, "Hello, Group A."

Nothing.

"Group A?"

Nothing.

Eustace grimaced at Lida, saying, "They're too busy building the castle to make a report." Into the walkie-talkie he said, "Come along, Group A. Somebody speak up."

Nothing.

At last getting nervous, Eustace said, "What's wrong there? Where are you? Group A! Group A! Herman!"

*

Drifting southward in a flat-bottom boat piled eight feet high with building blocks, nearing the intersection of Canal St. Denis with Canal de l'Ourcq, smiling in contentment, were Herman and Rudi and Otto. In Herman's hand was the walkie-talkie, and from it came the continuing voice of Eustace, with increasing panic, crying, "Rudi? Otto? Herman! Come *in!*"

Smiling, Herman extended his arm slowly out to the side, like a crane. He opened his fingers, and the walkie-talkie dropped from his hand into the canal.

The boat drifted on.

15

The heavy wooden door of the abandoned warehouse crashed open and Eustace thundered in on the motorcycle, with Lida cowering in the sidecar. Behind them, the Renault came spinning in, the frantic faces of Rosa and Angelo and Vito all visible through the windshield as they huddled together in the front seat. The two vehicles slid and scraped and squealed to a stop in front of the completed castle fragment, and Eustace and Lida hopped off the motorcycle as Rosa and Angelo and Vito burst out of the Renault.

"Herman!" yelled Eustace, uselessly. "Herman!"

"Germans!" roared Rosa, shaking her fists at the castle. "You can't trust Germans!"

Eustace looked at the orange truck, still in place on the other side of the warehouse, beyond the castle. "They left the truck," he said.

"Yes," said Rosa.

Angelo, who had run into the castle and then right back out again, joined them to say to Rosa, "They left the truck."

"I see it," Rosa told him. "It's not that hard to see."

Eustace, irritable with Italian being spoken around him, said, "What was that?"

"Angelo says," Rosa told him, "that the Germans left the truck."

"Oh."

Lida approached. "Look," she said. "They left the truck."

"So I'm told," said Eustace.

Angelo, irritable with English being spoken around him, said, "What was that?"

Rosa answered, "She says they left the truck."

Eustace said to Rosa, "What?"

"I was telling Angelo," Rosa said, "that Lida said they left the truck."

Joining the others, Vito sighed and said, "To think I could be in prison."

"Finally somebody says something I can understand," Angelo said, in deep annoyance, "and it's *that?*"

Eustace, no longer trusting anybody, peered hard at Angelo and Vito, saying, "What's that? What are they saying?"

Rosa said, "They're saying they left the truck."

Meanwhile, Angelo told Vito, "You notice they left the truck."

"But they didn't empty any blocks," Vito pointed out.

"That's right," Angelo said, looking around.

"What's that?" Eustace demanded. "That was something else."

Sighing, shaking her head, growing weary with the whole thing, Rosa said, "Vito says they didn't empty any blocks."

Eustace understood the import of that right away: "And yet they left the truck!" he shouted.

"I'm going back to Naples," Rosa said. "I'm not going to talk about trucks any more, I'm simply going back to Naples. That's it, that's all, I don't care, I'm going back."

"No, wait," Eustace said. "Vito has a point."

"I know, I know. They left the truck."

"Not that," Eustace said. "The point is, they took the blocks."

Rosa looked blank. "What?"

"There are no empty blocks here," Eustace explained. "So they had to have another truck to carry off all those blocks. There must be too many to fit in that little Volkswagen."

Rosa said, "But we don't know what the other truck looks like."

"No," said Eustace. "But we do know what the Volkswagen looks like. And we know which direction they'll go."

"East," said Rosa, looking grimmer. She was beginning to catch her second wind.

Lida, who had been looking from speaker to speaker, now said, "Does this mean the sweat of the people's brow has been stolen?"

"I couldn't have phrased it better myself," Eustace told her. "Wait in the sidecar."

At that point, the London taxicab came roaring through the open doorway, managed narrowly to avoid hitting the Renault and the motorcycle, and braked to a stop. Bruddy and Andrew and Sir Mortimer all leaped out, Bruddy shouting, "What's up? They copped it?"

"No time for explanations," Eustace told him. "The point is, they're gone, and they've got the loot in some other truck, still in the blocks. Look for their Volkswagen, with some other truck. We'll all head eastward, on different roads. Hurry! There's no time to lose!"

16

In shafts of sunlight before the reconstructed castle segment
dustmotes still hovered in the warehouse air, calling to mind
the hasty departure of Eustace and Lida and Rosa and Vito
and Angelo and Bruddy and Andrew and Sir Mortimer. And
once again the main warehouse doorway, left open in the
rush of events, framed an arrival; the bicycle built for two,
now bearing three. Renee peddled in back, Jean peddled in
front, and Charles as morose as a brooding chimpanzee
teetered on the handlebars.

A tricky question of balance arose as the bicycle slowed
to a stop, wobbling, pointing itself this way and that like
a nervous bird dog who's lost the scent, but no one actually
fell down. Charles, however, did have to invent one or two
new dance steps in his effort to get from handlebars to
ground without tipping over.

Freed at last of their bicycle, the three somberly surveyed
the scene, and it was Charles who spoke first, the cigarette
bobbing gloomily in the corner of his mouth as he said,
fatalistically, "So the Germans found it."

"You might know," Renee said, "they'd take it all for themselves."

Jean, already thinking ahead, pointed out, "They left the truck."

"We can use it," Charles said. "Better than the bicycle."

Renee looked more alert, her spirits lifting. "To follow them? Which way would they go?"

Jean shrugged: "To Germany."

"No," Charles said. "I don't think so."

Renee had been nodding in agreement with Jean; frowning at Charles she said, "Why not?"

There was a cold glint in Charles's eye now, a new lean toughness to his cheek. The professional thief was at work, all his knowledge and intuition brought into play. "If I were them," he said, more to himself than to the others, "where would I go?"

"Well, you wouldn't go to Germany," Renee said, "but that's because you're French."

Jean, his own expression becoming thoughtful, wandered away from the conversation, as Charles said, "Ah, but for the very reason that I *am* French, I very well might go to Germany. And for that exact same reason, I believe Herman and Rudi and Otto will remain right here in Paris."

Renee didn't begin to understand: "Why?"

"Consider the alternatives," Charles suggested. "Shall they go out on the highway and make a run for it, knowing we are all scant minutes behind them? Foolish."

"But if they stay in Paris, these Germans," Renee said, "*where* will they stay?"

"That's the problem," Charles admitted. "That's what I'm trying to comprehend, in my mind."

"Here!" suddenly called Jean. "Here, look at this!"

Charles and Renee looked around, to see Jean barely

visible on the far side of the truck. "Something else?" Charles asked, and he and Renee walked around the truck to see the Volkswagen beetle convertible tucked unobtrusively under the truck's wing. "Well, well," Charles said.

Unnecessarily, Jean said, "They left the car, too."

"Well, well, well, well, well," said Charles. He frowned at the car, thinking. Jean and Renee frowned at Charles, waiting. Charles frowned at the truck. Then he frowned at the constructed castle segment. Finally, with a more intense sort of frown, he frowned at the warehouse's rear windows. Renee, frowning at Charles's frowns, said, "Charles?"

"Mmm," said Charles.

Frowning encouragingly, Jean said, "Yes?"

"Hmmmmm," said Charles, and crossed the dirty floor to the nearest window and looked out.

Renee said, "Charles? What do you see?"

Charles turned back to the other two, and now his frown contained a smile inside it. "I see," he said, "a canal."

❁

Zipping northeastward out of Paris on the N 2, the Avenue Jean Jaurès through the suburbs of Aubervilliers and La Courneuve, the Renault skidded and slipped through the other traffic like a Gypsy knife through a merchant's ribcage. Rosa drove, with the abandon of a woman who has been assured by the Holy Virgin herself that no harm will befall her, while Angelo beside her stared and strained at every truck, every Volkswagen, every vehicle at all that they passed. And in the back seat, munching on his cheeks, calculating, deep in thought, ignoring the outside world, sat Vito.

131

"Bathtubs," muttered Rosa, slipping on two wheels between a Simca and a Citroën. "Bidets. Sinks. Toilets. And the *Germans* get the gold."

"Not for long," declared Angelo, staring for a millisecond into the astonished face of a chic woman whose Lamborghini Rosa had just forced off the road. "We'll catch up," Angelo vowed. "We'll catch up."

"Stop!" cried Vito.

Rosa spun around a tour bus, and did not stop.

"Stop!" repeated Vito. "Rosa, stop!"

"Why?"

"We have to go back!" Vito yelled, banging on the seat back. "Stop! Turn around!"

Angelo stared at him in disbelief. "But they're ahead of us!"

"No!" cried Vito. "They're in Paris!"

Rosa took her attention away from her driving long enough to glance at Vito in the rearview mirror and just miss seven vehicles. "In Paris?" she demanded. "In Paris?"

"Yes. When I know things," Vito said, "I know them, and I know I know this. They never left Paris. Turn around, Rosa. If you want to be a millionaire, turn around."

❈

"Group B!" yelled Eustace, steering the motorcycle one-handed as he strove to make contact with the remnants of his team. "Group B, I know you're out there! Come in!" And beside him Lida, white-faced but determined, clung to the sides of the sidecar and was given many opportunities to read the brand names on tires.

It was Bruddy's voice that finally responded to Eustace's screams, saying, "What now, you half a loaf? Did you find them?"

"No. Did you?"

"Not a whisker. This is a ruddy wild goose chase, if you ask me."

"Nobody asked you, Bruddy," Eustace said. Frustration made him snippish.

In the sidecar, Lida wailed, "We must find the people's money!"

"Yes, dear," Eustace said. "Yes, yes, we know."

And now from the B-marked walkie-talkie in Eustace's hand came Andrew's calm, rather thoughtful voice, saying, "You know, Eustace, I'm beginning to wonder if those chaps left Paris at all. Were it me, I believe I'd lie low in the city a while, and not involve myself in any merry chases."

"Hmmm," said Eustace. "Hmmmm."

17

Back into the warehouse, screeching to a stop near the empty truck and the incomplete castle, came the Renault. Rosa and Angelo and Vito surged out and ran in small circles, and then Angelo stopped and pointed and said, "Look! The bicycle!"

And there it was, leaning against the front of the truck. All three looked at it, and Vito said, "The French. They were here before us."

Rosa said, "But why leave their bicycle?"

"They didn't take the truck," Angelo pointed out.

Rosa gave him a look, but said nothing.

Vito sniffed. "I smell water," he said. "Not very clean water."

Rosa moved toward the rear windows: "What's outside here?"

*

On the Quai de Valmy, beside the Canal St. Martin just north of the Rue du Faubourg du Temple, where the canal goes underground beneath Boulevard Jules Ferry, Renee and Jean and Charles all stood up in the parked open-topped Volkswagen they'd commandeered at the warehouse, and gazed with some intensity at the canal. What they were watching so avidly was the slow but steady progress of the block-filled boat containing Herman and Rudi and Otto, moving in leisurely fashion away from them, southward. As they watched, the flat-bottom boat sailed serenely underground and out of sight.

Slowly, Charles and Jean and Renee all sat down, Charles in the driver's seat, Renee beside him, Jean in back. "Well," said Charles.

"Agreed," said Renee. "But what now?"

Thoughtfully Charles said, "This canal eventually goes on to the Seine. From there, they could very easily get out of Paris in any direction at all. I imagine that's their intention."

"Then let's get a boat," Renee said, "and follow them."

"No," Charles said. "They'd see us. We'll drive down to the other end of this tunnel, and wait for them."

Renee said, "Where's that?"

"Place de la Bastille. We'll see them come out there, and we'll trail them till they stop."

Jean said, "What if they turn around and come back out this way?"

Charles frowned at him. "Why would they do that?"

"They might," Jean insisted. "Maybe they intend just to hide in there until tonight, and then come out again and go back the other way."

Deadpan, Charles said, "Would you like to wait at this end, Jean, while Renee and I go keep watch at the Place de la Bastille?"

Smiling, Jean said, "And you'll come back for me if you get the money, won't you?"

Deadpan, Charles said, "Of course."

Suddenly, pointing at the canal, Renee said, "Look!"

They looked, and what they saw was Herman and Rudi and Otto *walking* out from the darkness of the tunnel, pacing carefully along the narrow path between the edge of the canal and the stone embankment wall.

"They're coming out," Renee said, unnecessarily.

"Without the boat," Charles pointed out.

"Ah," explained Jean.

＊

Pacing carefully along the narrow path between the edge of the canal and the stone embankment wall, Herman and Rudi and Otto walked in single file, talking over their shoulders to one another. Herman, in the lead, said, "Now we lie low for a few days, until the others wear themselves out with all their running around, and then we come back and collect our reward."

"I'm going to open a beer garden," Otto said. "In fact, a chain of beer gardens."

"There is," Herman said, the harsh planes of his face very nearly softening, "a small vineyard near Bernkastel, which I have coveted all my life. A fourteenth century castle stands atop the hill, overlooking the steep vine-covered slopes. There I will breed Doberman pinschers."

The three happy men climbed the narrow stone steps up to the Quai de Jemmapes, on the opposite side of the canal from their former colleagues, in their former Volkswagen. Otto said, "What about you, Rudi? You must have plans for your money."

"Oh, I do," Rudi said. He smiled like a suitcase opening.

"What, then?"

"Las Vegas," said Rudi.

Otto frowned at him. "What?"

"I have," Rudi said, "an absolutely unbeatable system at the craps table. I intend to win myself a casino." Preening a bit, smoothing down the wrinkles in his shirt, he said, "Can't you see me, running things in Las Vegas?"

"Possibly," Otto said.

"Taxi!" Herman said.

❋

The sound of water lapping against the stone wall of the abandoned warehouse was obliterated by the sudden putt-putt of a motorcycle and cough-cough of a London taxi. Then the engine sounds stopped, and the eternal water of the Canal St. Denis was heard again, gently lapping. Eustace's head appeared, with very wide eyes, in a window overlooking the canal. Eustace's head disappeared, with abruptness. The putt-putt and cough-cough burst once more into existence, and rapidly receded. The water lapped.

❋

Charles and Jean and Renee paced carefully along the narrow path between the edge of the Canal St. Martin and the stone embankment wall, reversing the route just taken by the departed Germans. Charles, in the lead, carried a small pocket flashlight, which he switched on as he reached the darkness of the tunnel.

"What an awful smell!" said Renee.

"Money sweetens all smells," suggested Jean.

Into the darkness they walked, wrinkling their noses against the aroma, blinking as Charles flashed his light here and there.

The flat-bottom boat was not very far from the entrance, tied to an old iron ring, and empty.

"Empty!" cried Renee.

Flashing the light around, Charles said, "They hid it somewhere." But the ranging beam of light showed nothing in particular; merely the slimy tunnel and the fetid water.

Jean said, "Would it all be underwater?"

Pointing the light down at the greenish water, Charles said, "Not even Herman would willingly reach in there."

"What did they *do* with it?" Renee cried, and her echo came back from the tunnel with a clear edge of panic in it. "They didn't carry it away, it must be *here*."

"There has to be an answer," Charles said. So fiercely was he concentrating that the cigarette stood out straight from the corner of his mouth, like a signpost. "There *has* to be an answer."

"I should hope so," said Jean.

But as Charles continued to shine the flashlight first this way and then that way, never seeing anything but the tunnel and the water, the water and the tunnel, the tunnel and the water and the empty boat, a sense of defeat gradually spread through all three of them, until Renee voiced what all three were thinking: "We can't find it. Whatever they did with it, we just can't find it."

Jean sighed.

"Very well," Charles said. His cigarette drooped, but his furrowed brow denoted determination. "We'll wait here," he said, "until they come back to get it. Then we'll follow them, and sooner or later we'll find an opportunity to take it away from them."

Jean sighed again, then coughed, then said, "Let us return to the outer world. I don't much like sighing in this atmosphere."

Discouraged, despondent, the three turned about and began to retrace their steps. But hardly had they taken half a dozen paces when Renee abruptly stopped and called, "Wait!"

The two men, who had been preceding her, halted and looked back, Charles shining his flashlight on Renee, who was pointing at the tunnel wall. "Look at this!" cried Renee.

The men did. Charles obligingly lit it with his flashlight beam. The wall was a wall, nothing more. It had no doors or other features. Jean said, "What about it?"

"This is it!" Renee told them.

They looked at her. Charles said, "This is what?"

"The *wall!*" Renee patted a palm against it. "This isn't the real wall, this is—"

Charles, suddenly understanding, reached out and poked at one of the wall's stone blocks. It moved. "You're right!"

Jean, at the edge of the false wall, pulled out a stone block and shook it. *Chinkle*. "This is it!"

"Now," Renee said. "Now what?"

"Now," Charles told her, "we reload the boat."

*

The white Renault racing south along the Quai de Valmy beside the Canal St. Martin had already passed the black Volkswagen—abandoned for the second time today—when Rosa at the wheel slammed on the brakes, causing Angelo to stuff much of himself into the map compartment under the dashboard and Vito to ricochet around the back seat like a captured firefly in a bottle. While Italian imprecations glittered in the Gallic air, Rosa shifted into reverse, slammed the Renault backward, and pounded it to a quivering halt beside the Volkswagen. Out bounded Rosa and Angelo. Out crawled Vito, shaking his head, counting his teeth.

Urchins nearby listlessly kicked a soccer ball in various directions. They listened to Rosa's Italianate French with a kind of passive bemusement, as though she weren't asking questions at all but were merely attempting to entertain them, until in a sudden fury Rosa grabbed the soccer ball and threatened to throw it into the canal; then it turned out that the urchins were capable of answering questions after all. Satisfied, Rosa kicked the ball a block away and, as the urchins ran screaming after it, turned to pass the information on to Angelo and Vito: "The Germans floated into that tunnel in a flat-bottomed boat stacked with building blocks. The Germans walked out and took a taxi away. Our French friends walked in, and didn't come back out."

"On!" cried Angelo.

"I've been a good man all my life," Vito mournfully announced, as the other two stuffed him back into the Renault. "Why am I being punished this way?"

＊

In the reeking tunnel, the refilled boat floated placidly southward, the way illuminated by Charles's tiny flashlight. Her voice echoing, Renee said, "Are you *sure* you're sure where this tunnel goes?"

Shrugging, Charles said, "It has to come out some time."

"You mean you *aren't* sure?"

"I'm sure," Charles told her. "Of course I'm sure. We'll come out just below the Place de la Bastille, I know that for a fact."

Renee sighed. The echo of her sigh circled the boat.

"Stealing from hotel rooms," she said, "is much more pleasant than this."

"After today," Jean told her, encouragingly, "you'll be able to *live* in a hotel."

She looked at him in astonishment: "And be robbed?"

Peering ahead, Charles said, "I think I see light at the end of the tunnel."

Renee squinted: "Where?"

"Turn off the light," Jean said, "so we can see."

"Right."

Charles switched off the flashlight. There was utter pitch blackness, total ebony, midnight, thoroughgoing stygian dark. Great furry gobs of black, in which the miasma of the water seemed to roll up around them, as though only the feeble flashlight had held horror and evil and catastrophe at bay.

"*Turn it on!*" Renee screamed.

The light flicked on, pale, uncertain, but at least real. "Sorry," said Jean. "I thought I saw light at the end of the tunnel."

"Don't do that again," Renee said.

✱

Beside the doubly abandoned Volkswagen stood the motorcycle and the London taxi. Beside the motorcycle stood Eustace, obstinately clutching the soccer ball while engaged in frantic furious sign-language converse with the urchins.

✱

Charles switched off the flashlight. "There, you see? Light at the end of the tunnel."

"Thank God," said Renee.

The boat floated toward the arched exit. Beyond, sunlight gleamed on the water of the Gare de l'Arsenal, the last step in the canal journey before the Seine.

"I told you I was sure," Charles said. "That's the Boulevard Bourdon over there. We're passing right under the Place de la Bastille."

"Just so we're coming out," Renee said, and out they came, and sunlight gleamed on their faces.

✿

Leaning over the railing on the south side of the Place de la Bastille, Rosa and Angelo and Vito looked down at the sunlit faces of Renee and Charles and Jean, who failed to recognize their Italian friends silhouetted against the sky above them. "We could drop something on them," Rosa said, conversationally. "Like an airplane, like a bomber. We could sink them from here."

"No, no," Angelo said. "We don't want to sink our profits."

Vito said, "Why couldn't *they* get the bathtubs? It isn't fair."

✿

In their hotel room, the triumphant Germans poured more drinks, but while Herman actually gulped his down both Otto and Rudi were more circumspect about their alcoholic intake, Otto surreptitiously emptying his glass into a long-suffering plant and Rudi just as surreptitiously emptying his out the window. What a waste of good liquor.

✿

Within the tunnel lately occupied by Renee and Charles and Jean and the loot from the castle there was a mighty *roaring*, preceded by a stabbing, prying white light. The *roaring* advanced and became the motorcycle, without its sidecar, racing along the narrow path beside the wall. A grim-faced Bruddy clung to the handlebars, while a white-faced Eustace on the seat behind him clung to Bruddy's waist. Quick, urgent, determined, *loud*, the motorcycle roared on.

*

Andrew, in terror of the French traffic, steered the London taxi timidly southward along the busy Boulevard Richard Lenoir. Sir Mortimer and Lida sat in back, a large map of the city spread out on their laps. "For God's sake, Andrew," Sir Mortimer cried, while Lida tentatively moved her fingers this way and that on the map, "get some speed up!"

"I'm not a driver," Andrew said, quailing away from several blatting little deux chevaux. "Bruddy's the driver."

"Get your *hands* out of there!" Sir Mortimer cried, slapping at Lida's fingers. "I can't *see!*"

"But I think we're here," Lida said, her fingers all over the place again.

"Out! Out! Away!" Successfully repelling Lida's fingers, Sir Mortimer peered at the map, saying, "The only other bit of water I see is down here by the Place de la Bastille. Are you on Boulevard Richard Lenoir?"

"I haven't the faintest notion," Andrew said. "Frankly, I think I'm in hell."

"Young woman," Sir Mortimer said, "would you *kindly* keep your hands to yourself?"

"I'm sorry, I'm only trying to—"

"Make yourself useful," Sir Mortimer suggested. "Find a street sign."

"If only," Andrew said forlornly, "I had used my talents for good."

❖

Herman and Rudi and Otto, (apparently) done in by schnapps, sat sprawled and (apparently) asleep in their hotel room. Slowly, Rudi's left eyelid raised, his left eye scanned back and forth like a TV monitor. Slowly he lifted his head, cautiously he surveyed his companions. Slowly he got to his feet, slowly he crept from the room.

❖

On the comparatively broad waterway of the Gare de l'Arsenal, the loot-laden boat flowed serenely toward the Seine. Renee and Charles and Jean, much more cheerful and optimistic now that they were free of the reeking tunnel, smiled happily at one another and at the busy, tooting, merry, ebullient life of Paris all around them.

"Well, Charles," Renee said, basking in the sun, "what should we do now?"

"We'll go to Ile St. Louis," Charles told her, "we'll hide the blocks there, and then we'll lie low until all the foreigners go away."

"We don't have to lie low," Jean said.

The other two looked at him. Charles said, "Why not?"

With a coy smile, Jean said, "*We* didn't doublecross anybody. The Germans did it all. We've been out looking for them, like everybody else."

A slow smile spread across Charles's face. "That's nice," he said. "That's very nice."

*

In the Renault, driving along the Boulevard Bourdon, Rosa and Angelo and Vito watched the progress of the flat-bottom boat. "Look at them smile," Angelo said. "Just look at the bastards smile."

"They'll smile," Rosa said. "They'll smile upside down, before this day is done.

*

Otto, opening a cautious eye, looked at where Rudi wasn't, and in utter shock he jumped to his feet and stared around the room. Herman slept on. Rudi was gone.

So, a minute later, was Otto.

*

The walkway at the east side of the tunnel under Boulevard Richard Lenoir comes to an abrupt end where the tunnel empties into the Gare de l'Arsenal. Unfortunately, Bruddy didn't know this until it was too late.

"Look, Mama!" cried a young child from Kuwait, tugging at its mother's sleeve. But of course, adults never look in time, and so the mother failed to see the motorcycle come roaring and flying out of the tunnel, its headlight glaring uselessly in sunlight, its wheels racing uselessly in midair. She failed to see the motorcycle arch out high over the water. She failed to see the two men aboard the motorcycle frantically wave their arms and legs in their struggle

145

to climb up sunbeams to safety. And she failed to see the motorcycle and its passengers knife down into the water and sink like a stone. All she saw, in fact, was a faint rippling of the heavy oily water. "You're overtired, dear," she told her child, as the child tried vainly to explain the sight that had just been missed. "Too much sightseeing," the mother decided, and took herself and her child straightaway back to the hotel.

18

Along the Quai de Jemmapes, at the northern end of the
water tunnel, strolled an innocent bystander, enjoying the
day and the view and minding his own business, until all
at once Rudi, enraged, came dashing out of the tunnel,
thundered up the stone steps from the canal, grabbed the
innocent bystander by the lapels, and screamed in German
into the poor fellow's astonished face, "You've got my
blocks!"

"Help!" said the innocent bystander. "Help! Help!"

What might have happened to the innocent bystander
next is conjectural, as this was the moment when a small
taxi arrived on the scene and Otto hopped out, crying, "So!"

"You!" yelled Rudi, releasing the innocent bystander,
who at once went home and locked himself in a closet, while
Rudi transferred his lapel-clutching to Otto. "It was *you!*"

But Otto was also clutching lapels; Rudi's lapels. And
Otto was yelling, "You would, would you? You think you'll
get it all yourself, do you?"

"What did you do with them?" Rudi demanded, shaking

Otto by the lapels in exactly the same way that Otto was shaking *him* by the lapels.

It was Otto who first noticed the redundancy in their actions. As bewilderment overtook anger in his expression, he said, "Rudi? What?"

"You've got to split with me," Rudi insisted. "I'm the one brought you into this."

"Split with you? What are you talking about?"

"Where are the blocks?"

The blocks?" Otto blinked past Rudi toward the canal and the tunnel. "*I* don't have anything. I just got here."

"Then who did it?" Rudi demanded.

"Who did—" Blood drained from Otto's face. "They're gone? The blocks are *gone?*"

"Of course they're gone!"

"But— Rudi, are you sure?"

"Would I lie to you?" Rudi asked.

Rather than answer such a question, Otto tore himself from Rudi's lapel-grabbing grasp and ran down the steps and into the tunnel. Rudi, an instant later, followed, pulling his flashlight from his pocket.

Both men pounded into the tunnel, and came to a stop where last they had built the castle wall. Rudi shone his light: "There. You see?"

Otto stared, then in sudden fury turned and clutched at Rudi. "You! It's you!"

"No no no!" Rudi shouted, fending him off. "Would I still be here? Would I be so *upset?*"

"No one else knew about it," Otto pointed out.

"Herman! It was Herman!"

Otto shook his head. "He was still asleep when I left."

"Then," Rudi said, "it has to be either you or me, and I know it isn't me."

"But it *has* to be you," Otto said.

A crunching sound behind them made both men look toward the entrance of the tunnel, where a bum had just come stumbling in, looking for a quiet place to nap with a bottle of wine. Otto and Rudi stared at him. The bum continued to mooch along for a few paces, then became aware of the two men so fervently surveying him. He gave them a drunken nod and smile, and started to bend in several places, preparatory to sitting on the path. Then he paused, shaped like a letter in the Arab alphabet, becoming dimly aware of the waves of menace sweeping in his direction. Trying to focus on Rudi and Otto, he slowly straightened again and, increasingly nervous, shuffled away.

"It's him," Rudi said, watching the bum retreat to sunlight. "I know it's him, look how guilty his shoulders are."

"No, Rudi," Otto said. "If he'd taken everything away, why would he come back?"

"It's him, I tell you."

"No, it isn't," Otto said, and sighed. "But it's somebody like him," he said. "Someone saw us hide it all here, and waited for us to leave, and took it all away."

With a defeated nod, Rudi said, "You're right. I know you're right."

"So it's gone forever."

Rudi shook his head. "I was going to write such a beautiful will."

"And we'd better be gone forever, too," Otto added.

Rudi frowned at him. "What? Why?"

"Sooner or later," Otto said, "Herman will come back here. Do you want to wait here and try to convince him you're innocent?"

Rudi looked startled. "No," he said. "Herman? No, I'm a bleeder."

"Then let's go," Otto said.

Frightened, but grimly determined, Rudi said, "No. I can't give up."

"I can," Otto said. "I'm going back to Germany.

"Good luck," Rudi told him.

'No," Otto said. All I need is a train ticket. *You're* the one who needs the good luck. Say hello to Herman for me." And with a small salute, Otto trudged away.

For a moment longer, Rudi stood looking around, shining his flashlight deeper into the tunnel. The boat was gone. The loot was gone. Rudi sighed, he shook his head, but his expression was still determined when at last he tramped away.

19

"Get on with it, man!" cried Sir Mortimer, from the back seat of the London taxi. "For God's sake, get on with it!"

Into the traffic pattern of the Place de la Bastille, a somewhat smaller version of the Arc de Triomphe with only ten separate streets serving as spokes to this hub, wobbled the coughing black taxi, with Andrew still miserably at the wheel. "They're insane," Andrew babbled. "They're all insane."

"Turn the wheel!" cried Sir Mortimer. "Get us *out* of here!"

Traffic flashed by on all sides. Horns sounded, brakes squealed. Lida, on her knees on the floor in the back of the cab, prayed loudly to the Blessed Virgin, in Spanish. And, more by luck than intent, Andrew steered the taxi away from the Bastille monument and onto the appropriate street for them, being the Boulevard Bourdon, running southward down the west side of the Gare de l'Arsenal.

"Over there!" cried Sir Mortimer, pointing toward two sopping figures clambering up into view from the canal. "Stop over there!"

"Stop?" Andrew echoed. "Oh, if only I could!"

But he could, and did. The taxi bunked into the curb, and slowed, and stalled, and stopped. And Eustace and Bruddy, both dripping wet, came across the sidewalk and entered the cab, Bruddy taking the wheel as Andrew gratefully slid over to the other side, and Eustace joining Sir Mortimer and Lida in back.

"What a day," Eustace said. "Stop praying, Lida, I'm all right."

In front, Andrew said, "What's that awful smell?"

"Me," said Bruddy, dangerously. "You can smell like it, too, if you just jump in the canal."

To Eustace, Sir Mortimer said, "Good God, man, you didn't have to swim."

"I did," Eustace said, "after our friend Bruddy sank the motorcycle. Any sign of our quarry?"

"I haven't been able to look," Sir Mortimer said, "with all this traffic."

Eustace said, "I thought Andrew was driving."

"I was," Andrew said. "And I never will again, I assure you. If I had a license, I'd rip it up."

Sir Mortimer blanched: "You don't have a license?"

Ignoring all that, Eustace said, "They have to be farther on. Drive, Bruddy, and try to stay out of the canal this time."

Andrew said, "Would you all mind terribly, Eustace, if you came up here and I got in back?"

Eustace frowned. "Why?"

Sir Mortimer said, "To concentrate the aroma, I suppose. The suggestion has its merits."

"All right, all right," Eustace said. "But then let's get on with it."

The exchange was made, Sir Mortimer ostentatiously closed the glass partition between the front and back seats,

Eustace and Bruddy opened their side windows all the way, and at last they drove on, traveling south past the Gare de l'Arsenal right down to the Seine, where they stopped at the Pont Morland, the bridge under which the canal at last empties into the river. All five climbed out of the cab and went to the railing to look left and right along the Seine. To the right were the two islands in the middle of Paris—the Ile St. Louis nearest and the Ile de la Cité beyond it—while to the left was the open river, extending away more or less straight under its bridges to the city line and beyond. And in neither direction, among the boats and barges of the river traffic, was there to be seen anywhere a flat-bottom boat piled high with building blocks.

"Ah, dear," Andrew said. "We've lost them."

"Well, we've got to find them, Eustace said. "They can't have gotten far, not yet."

Sir Mortimer said, "But which way? Assuming they tied up somewhere along the river, which direction did they go?"

Eustace said, "We'll have to split up."

He got a number of cold looks for that, and Bruddy said, with deceptive softness, "Oh, we will, will we?"

"It's the only sensible way," Eustace insisted. "Can't we trust one another?"

"Certainly not," Sir Mortimer said, as though someone had just insulted him.

Unexpectedly, Andrew took Eustace's part, saying, "But we *can* trust one another. We few British."

"I've heard," Bruddy said, "of Brits what couldn't trust one another. Once or twice I've heard such things."

"But surely there's enough loot for us all," Andrew said. "I mean, for those of us right here."

"Of course there is," Eustace said. "And if we *all* go off in the wrong direction, how does that help anyone?"

"All right," Bruddy said to Eustace. "You go off with Andrew here, and I'll stick with Sir Mortimer."

Doubtful, Andrew said, "Is that best?"

"Whatever you want is fine with me," Eustace said.

"Perhaps," Andrew said, "those of us who have been in the canal should form one group, and those of us who haven't been in the canal should form the other."

"Hear hear," said Sir Mortimer.

"Fine," Eustace said. "Bruddy, you'll come with me."

"I suppose so," Bruddy said, and turned a gimlet eye on Andrew and Sir Mortimer. "Just remember," he said, "I know you both, very well."

"Of course, Bruddy," said Sir Mortimer, with an encouraging smile. "And Andrew and I know you."

"We'll leave the car here," Eustace said, "and meet back here in an hour."

"Very good," said Andrew.

Pointing away toward the Ile St. Louis, Eustace said, "We'll go that way, you go the other. Come along, Lida."

And the intrepid band became two intrepid bands, one of which smelled bad.

20

Renee and Charles and Jean, constructing a low wall at the waterline on the south side of the Ile St. Louis, were unaware of the three interested observers on Pont de Sully, the nearby bridge. "They're sloppier builders than the Germans," commented Vito.

"The wall doesn't have to last very long," Rosa pointed out. "Only until they're out of sight."

"They're finished," Angelo said.

Below, Renee and Charles and Jean, with much hand-shaking and smiling and back-slapping, had indeed finished their wall. Leaving the boat tied to it, they made their way up a nearby flight of steps onto the island and disappeared into the crowded tangle of ancient buildings there.

"Now," Angelo said, "it's our turn."

"We put it all back in the boat," Rosa said.

"No," said Vito. "I'm not a turtle, I stay on dry land. We want a truck."

"Yes, a truck," agreed Angelo. "Much better."

"All right," said Rosa. "You two go get one."

Both men considered her. Vito said, "What about you?"

"Someone has to stand guard," she said, reasonably enough. "In case the Frenchmen come back and move it again."

The two men continued to consider her. Rosa looked back at them in amazement, and said, "You don't trust *me?*"

"No," said Angelo.

"Not for a second," said Vito.

"But what could *I* do," Rosa demanded, "a mere woman, with all those heavy blocks, all by myself?"

Vito and Angelo thought that over, looking at one another out of the corners of their eyes. Finally, they both shrugged in agreement. "All right," Angelo said. "But we won't be long, Rosa."

"That's right," Rosa said. "You should hurry."

Vito said, "Oh, we will. Rely on it."

Deadpan, Rosa watched the two men hurry away.

*

Loping, Herman entered the tunnel where much earlier today he had last seen the booty. He stopped, he gazed about at emptiness, and somehow he seemed to grow both taller and thinner, his harsh cheekbones gleaming with a pale light all their own. Raising his arms like a vampire bat, he spoke two thundering words, which echoed and reverberated forever inside the tunnel: "OTTO! RUDI!"

Turning about, Herman loped away.

*

Vito and Angelo paused near a trucking company parking lot just off the Quai Henri IV. "You wait here," Angelo said, "I'll go in and get us a truck."

"Why don't we go in together?"

"Two people would attract too much attention. Don't worry, I'll be right back. You can watch the gate."

"I will," Vito promised. "I'll be waiting."

Angelo hurried away.

*

Returning to the London taxi, morose and depressed, having been assured by several English-speaking tourists that no flat-bottom boat piled high with building blocks had traveled eastward along the Seine this afternoon, Andrew and Sir Mortimer plodded along in silence until Andrew, spotting the taxi, said, "The others aren't back yet."

"I am becoming," Sir Mortimer said, "profoundly gloomy. Profoundly."

"Look!" said Andrew, suddenly pointing.

Sir Mortimer looked, and now they both saw the same thing: strolling this way, chatting happily together, were Jean and Charles and Renee.

"Hi!" called Andrew, trotting forward, Sir Mortimer in his wake. "Hi! You there!"

Charles, looking up from an extremely pleasant discussion to see the two Englishmen hurrying his way, was about to turn tail and run when Jean grabbed his arm with a warning hiss, saying, "Wait! They don't know we took it."

"Ah," said Charles, and at once he pasted a welcoming smile to his face and even waved a little wave.

Arriving, out of breath, Andrew cried, "Thank heaven we found you! The Germans stole the goods!"

His face richly expressive of shock, Jean said, "No!"

"We've trailed them," Sir Mortimer said, "down the canal as far as the river. They have all the blocks in a small boat."

Andrew said, "Have you seen them?"

Innocent, Jean said, "The Germans?" Then he turned to translate into French for the benefit of Charles and Renee. "They want to know if we've seen the Germans, in a small boat."

Wide-eyed, curious and concerned, both Charles and Renee solemnly shook their heads, while Andrew and Sir Mortimer watched. Then Jean, still in French, said, "I am now explaining to you that the Germans found the loot and betrayed us all. You are now becoming shocked."

Charles and Renee became shocked. "Terrible! Terrible!" cried Charles. "I may faint!" cried Renee.

Switching to English, Jean said, "This is terrible news, gentlemen. Whatever shall we do about it?"

Waving in the direction of Ile St. Louis, Sir Mortimer said, "Eustace and Bruddy and the Lida woman are searching off in that direction."

Trying to hide his sudden worry, Jean said, "You think the Germans might have gone that way?"

Pointing to from whence they had just come, Andrew said, "They certainly didn't go over there."

"Well," Jean said, "if I were the Germans, I think I'd go over to the Left Bank and transfer the loot to a truck."

Excited, Andrew said, "You might be right!"

"Yes," Jean said. "Why don't you two look over there, and Renee and Charles and I will check down toward the Ile St. Louis, just to be on the safe side."

"You come with us," Sir Mortimer said.

"Oh, I should stay with my own group," Jean said, "don't you think?"

"No," Andrew said, "that's a very good idea. You can translate for us."

"Then we'll all go together," Jean said.

"No," Sir Mortimer said. "Charles and Renee can check that island, and we three will do the other side of the river."

Unable to think of an argument against this plan, and afraid to hesitate too long, Jean said unhappily, "Very well. That's what we'll do then."

"Good," said Sir Mortimer. "Off we go."

Turning to Charles and Renee, and switching to French, Jean said, "I have to go with them. You are supposedly checking the Ile St. Louis, while we check the Left Bank."

With a little smile, Charles said, "The Ile St. Louis? We'll be happy to check it."

"I'm sure," Jean said meaningfully, "I can trust you both."

Renee, with her most girlish smile, replied, "But of course, Jean."

"Come along, come along," Sir Mortimer said. "We're wasting time."

"Yes, certainly," said Jean.

Sir Mortimer and Jean and Andrew moved off toward the cab, Sir Mortimer saying, "Jean, you drive."

"Certainly," said Jean.

Charles and Renee smiled at one another.

*

Rosa was just completing the job of refilling the boat with blocks when Angelo, out of breath but dangerous-looking, came down the steep narrow steps and loomed over her. She didn't see him until he said, with deceptive pleasantness, "How good of you to do all that work and not even ask for help."

Rosa jumped with fright, nearly falling out of the boat. "Oh! Angelo! You startled me."

159

"No doubt," said Angelo.

Quickly recovering, Rosa said, "I changed my mind about the truck."

"So I see."

"I thought I might as well go ahead and load all this while waiting for you to come back."

"Yes, indeed."

Rosa, rather nervous, looked past Angelo up the steps: "Where's Vito?"

Angelo smiled. "Would you like to wait for him?"

Rosa hesitated, considering the options. Angelo continued to smile down at her, until at last she returned his smile, saying, "Vito can catch up with us later."

"Of course," said Angelo, as he stepped down into the boat.

21

Vito, at the head of the narrow steps on the Ile St. Louis, gazed forlonly down at where the boat and the wall of loot had so recently been. Words, even in Italian, failed him, and at last he turned away, just as Charles and Renee came smiling and laughing and hurrying around the corner.

Bump. Stare. Mutual understanding.

Charles pushed past Vito, staring down at the water at the foot of the steps. Behind him, Renee's agonized voice said, "Charles? Is it—?"

Instead of answering, Charles turned and grabbed Vito in both hands, shaking him and yelling in his face, "Where is it? What have you done with it?"

Maintaining as much dignity as possible while being shaken like a maraca, Vito declaimed, "Unhand me, you big crook."

"Don't speak Italian at me, you miserable worm!"

"Charles!" wailed Renee, from the top of the steps. "Charles, they've taken it all!"

Still clutching to Vito, Charles said to Renee, "He'll tell me, or by heaven—"

Struggling in Charles's iron grip, Vito yelled, "Release me, you baboon!"

"*He* doesn't have it," Renee said. "He wouldn't be here if he did."

Charles frowned, thinking about that.

"Let me go," Vito announced, "or I shall be forced to strike you!"

"But if this old turd doesn't have the goods," Charles said, "who does?"

"The other Italians," suggested Renee. "Rosa and Angelo."

Recognizing the names out of the gabble of French, Vito jumped up and down excitedly in Charles's hands, yelling, "Yes! Yes! Rosa and Angelo! They robbed us all!"

Nodding, releasing Vito, turning away from him as though he'd ceased to exist, Charles said to Renee, "Yes, you're right. They must have followed us, the way we followed the Germans."

"And doublecrossed Vito along with the rest of us," said Renee.

Vito now clutched at Charles, trying to attract his attention again, saying, "Rosa. Rosa and Angelo, we have to find them."

Distractedly pushing Vito off, Charles said, "We have to find them."

"Yes, Charles," Renee said. "Think. Think."

The three of them moved slowly away from the steps, Charles thoughtful, Renee watching Charles, Vito darting around them like a frantic puppy.

22

Andrew, Sir Mortimer, and Jean walked back to the taxicab, now parked on the Quai St. Bernard on the Left Bank. Andrew and Sir Mortimer were both gloomy again, and Jean was also trying to simulate gloom. Jean it was who said, as they reached the taxi, "Well, we seem to have lost them for good."

"Most unsporting," Andrew said. "Most unfortunate."

"I did not come all this way," Sir Mortimer said, "to be made a fool of by Germans."

"I know how you feel, Sir Mortimer," Jean said, "but what are we to do?"

"Keep searching!"

"I'm afraid," Jean said, with a Gallic shrug, "I don't have your English sinew. I am prepared at this point to abandon all hope."

Suddenly suspicious, Sir Mortimer frowned at the Frenchman: "You're giving it up, are you?"

"I'm afraid so," said Jean. "It has been a pleasure working with all of you, gentlemen, and only unfortunate that our high hopes have been dashed, but now that the inevitable hour of parting has come upon us—" And he extended his hand for a round of farewell shakes.

"Just one moment, there," Sir Mortimer said.

Affable, innocent, Jean said, "Beg pardon?"

Andrew was also now frowning at Jean. To Sir Mortimer he said. "There's something amiss about this Slyboots."

"Precisely what I was thinking," said Sir Mortimer.

Backing away, Jean continued his friendly smile as he said, "Well, I must be off. Au revoir. You needn't offer me a lift, I have friends quite close by—"

Sir Mortimer and Andrew moved after Jean, who backpedaled more rapidly. "Here!" said Sir Mortimer. "Stop a moment there!"

"Hold on, now," Andrew said.

Abandoning smile and all other pretense, Jean turned and ran. Sir Mortimer and Andrew pelted after him.

✻

Having fruitlessly crossed Ile St. Louis, Eustace and Bruddy and Lida were now looking fruitlessly riverward from the Pont St. Louis, the bridge between the two islands. "Nothing," Eustace said bitterly, and turned to see Vito and Charles and Renee trotting in his direction. "Vito!" Eustace cried in astonishment. "What's happened?"

Racing toward Eustace, while Charles and Renee exchanged a nonplussed glance in the background, Vito cried out, "Where's Rosa? Where's Angelo? Have you seen them?"

"*More* Italian!" cried Eustace.

Meanwhile, seeing no point in fleeing, Charles and Renee had also approached, and Charles said, "What are all you people doing here?"

"And more French!" cried Eustace.

The multiplicity of languages apparently caused something to snap inside Lida, who abruptly shouted out in Spanish, "The people's money has been stolen!"

Simultaneously, Bruddy, in his version of English, was asking, "Where'd you lot come from?"

And now, briefly, everyone spoke at once, in a variety of tongues, until Eustace screamed, "*Stop!*" They all stopped, startled by the shout, and Eustace told them, "I've had enough! I can't stand it any more!" Panting, struggling to regain control of himself, he said, "All right. Now we'll find out what's happening." To Vito, speaking slowly and carefully and loudly, with elaborate hand gestures, he said, "Where's Rosa? Rosa!"

And Vito replied with terrific excitement, "Yes, yes, Rosa! She stole everything!"

Eustace waggled his hands, crying, "Wait, wait, wait! Go slowly."

"You idiot," Charles said, "can't you understand? The Italians stole it all!"

To Charles, Eustace said, "Will you wait? I'm having trouble enough not understanding Italian, without having to not understand French. Do you mind?"

Lida said, "Perhaps I could try in Spanish."

"We're standing here," Vito said, "having a tea party, and our money's gone!"

To Vito, Eustace said, "Will you *wait?*"

"French and Italian and Spanish are all very close," Lida pointed out, "so perhaps I could—"

"Ah!" said Eustace, clutching at straws. "Try it! Ask Vito, uh— What do I want to ask him?"

Bruddy said, "Where the flippin Germans are."

"Yes," Eustace said. "Exactly. Where are the Germans?"

To Vito, in her South American Spanish, Lida said, "Where are the Germans?"

In some astonishment, Vito said, "Are you talking to me?"

"The people from Germany," Lida said.

"That's not Italian you're talking," Vito told her. "Even in Sicily that wouldn't be Italian."

Eustace said, "What's he saying?"

Shaking her head, Lida said, "I'm sorry. I don't know."

"If you people," Charles said, "are deciding something, I want to know what it is."

Pointing at Charles, Eustace said to Lida, "Try it on him."

"All right." Approaching Charles, Lida said in Spanish, "The Germans. They stole the people's money."

Appalled, Charles said, "Good God, what a noise."

Renee said, "I think it's Spanish."

To Lida, hopefully, Eustace said, "What are they saying?"

"Something in French."

"I *know* it's in French!"

Becoming even more excited, now that no one was talking to him, Vito cried, "We must *do* something! Stop all the talk and *do* something!"

Renee said to Charles, "They're deciding something behind our backs."

Glowering at everybody, Bruddy said, "I'd like to take up a stick and just start laying about me."

Vito then started yelling at Eustace while Charles started talking tough in the general direction of Bruddy. Eustace and Bruddy replied in kind, while Renee shouted alternately at Charles and Bruddy. Lida appealed to everyone in a combination of Spanish and English. A general ruckus developed, in which all six shouted and nobody listened, and none of the six noticed the flat-bottom boat piled high with building blocks as it eased slowly around the end of Ile St. Louis and moved underneath the bridge on which they pranced and danced, heading now north toward the Right Bank.

It was Lida who first saw the boat, with its two cheerfully oblivious occupants, moving away northward from the bridge, but it was quite some time before she could attract the attention of all the other screaming combatants. She caught Renee's eye first, then she and Renee captured Eustace and forced him to look at the departing boat, and at last the other three gave off their insults and imprecations, and a great silence settled on them all as they watched the boat glide on.

It was Eustace who broke the silence, with sudden efficient determination, saying, "Right. We've got it now. We'll follow them. Bruddy, you take the Frenchman and go along the Right Bank. I'll—"

"Oh, no, you don't," Bruddy said. "We don't split up, not any more."

Impatient, Eustace said, "You can trust *me*, Bruddy, I'm the one organized this scheme. We *have* to split up. What if we all stay on the island, and they off-load the lolly on the Right Bank?"

"We'll hurry over," Bruddy said. "All together-like."

"And we'll be too late," Eustace pointed out. "They'll slip through our fingers."

As Bruddy thought that over, frowning, Renee said quietly to Charles, "Can we at all get away from these people?"

"Not yet. We'll need them to help with the Italians. Later, though."

"All right," Bruddy finally decided. "We split up, for the nonce. But you try a fast one, my lad, and you'll be ever so sorry."

"I've been sorry most of the day," Eustace told him.

23

Dejected and footsore, Andrew and Sir Mortimer returned to the London taxi, having failed miserably in their attempt to overtake the fleet-footed Jean. "I must say," Andrew commented, limping, "I'm not the runner I used to be."

"I never was," Sir Mortimer said, grumpily. "I have always despised athletics."

They reached the cab, and as Andrew's hand touched the door handle three caped gendarmes were suddenly among them; all around them, in fact; surrounding them, in fact. Andrew and Sir Mortimer, startled out of their funk, gaped at the gendarmes. "Yes?" said Sir Mortimer. "May I assist you?"

One of the gendarmes, at least, spoke English. "This is," he asked, "your autocar?"

Irritable, Sir Mortimer said, "Yes, of course it is. Just give us the ticket and we'll move on."

"Ticket?" With a sad smile, the gendarme shook his head. "We do not talk about a ticket," he said. "This, as it happens, is a thieved autocar."

Sir Mortimer and Andrew looked blankly at one another. Then they looked blankly at the London taxicab. Then they looked blankly at the gendarmes.

"No," said Andrew, "I'm afraid not. I couldn't run another step."

Forcefully Sir Mortimer told the gendarmes, "There *is* an explanation."

With sudden wild hope, Andrew looked at his confederate: "There is?"

Politely the gendarmes waited. Slowly the stern expression on Sir Mortimer's face crumbled into despair. "But I'll be blowed," he said at last, "if I can find one."

24

On the Quai de la Mégisserie, on the Right Bank of the Seine, Bruddy and Charles and Renee leaned on the railing and looked across the sparkling water to the Ile de la Cité, where the walled boat had just come to a stop at another narrow flight of stone steps. Rosa and Angelo, tying the boat in place, seemed to be involved in a not-entirely-friendly debate, though they were too far away for Bruddy and Charles and Renee to hear their voices.

"Now we've got you, sweethearts," Bruddy said. "If only that bloody Eustace gets there in time."

"Our friend," pointed out Renee, "is speaking English again."

"It seems habitual with him," Charles said. "But pay no attention; he will soon cease to be a nuisance to us."

Frowning at them, Bruddy said, "What are you two plotting? You're up to something."

Across the water, the debate seemed at last to have resolved itself; Rosa and Angelo climbed the steps together, leaving the boat tied up behind them. Half a dozen steps, and they were out of sight.

"Good," said Charles. To Bruddy he said, "Come along, before your friend Eustace doublecrosses us." And he trotted off in the direciton of the nearest bridge, the Pont Neuf.

Bruddy, not having understood what had just been said to him, was startled and not at all pleased when first Charles and then Renee took to their heels, running away from him. "Here!" he shouted, haring off after them. "Hi! Come back! What you trying to pull?"

Very quickly Bruddy overtook the trotting Charles, grabbed him by the arm, and began to wrestle with him. Charles, bewildered and angry, naturally defended himself, shouting, "What are you doing? We've got to get over there!"

Bruddy had a good grip, and wasn't about to let go: "Try to run out on *me*, will you?"

Renee ran in little circles around the combatants, screaming, "Stop! Stop! Have you gone crazy?"

"We've got to get the loot!" Charles yelled. "They'll get away with the loot!" he repeated, at the top of his voice, and only then did he become aware of the three gendarmes standing at the curb, attracted by the fracas.

The change in Charles's reaction alerted Bruddy, who looked over his shoulder and also saw the gendarmes, smiling, calm, observing, patiently awaiting their turn to enter the conversation.

"Um," said Bruddy, and released Charles, and stood there smoothing down his jacket and shirt.

The gendarmes approached. Pleasantly, one of them said to Charles, "And what is it we are fighting about, on such a lovely day?"

"Um," said Charles, in French.

" 'Loot?' " quoted a second gendarme. "Was there a reference to 'loot'?"

"Alas," said Charles.

25

Eustace, Vito, and Lida, prowling the Ile de la Cité, had first
discovered Rosa and Angelo in the process of stealing a
truck. Themselves remaining out of sight, they had followed
the truck thieves back to the Quai de l'Horloge, where the
boat was tied up, and now from a nearby vantage point they
watched their two former allies unload all the building blocks
from the boat, carry them up the steps, and load them into
the back of the truck. Eustace observed all this with the
purest of pleasure, Vito with extremely mixed feelings, and
Lida kept looking about in apprehension, finally saying,
"Where are the others? Renee, and Charles, and Bruddy?"

Delighted as much by their absence as by the blocks'
presence, Eustace smiled and said, "I really couldn't say."

"Perhaps something has happened to them."

Trying without success to look sad, Eustace agreed:
"It is possible."

Continuing to look around, Lida suddenly lit up, saying,
"Oh, look! Here're Jean and Rudi!"

Startled, anything but pleased, Eustace whipped
around, and by God it was true. Here came Jean and Rudi,

an unlikely couple at the best of times, both smiling. Lida echoed their smile, but Eustace and Vito both looked rather glum as Jean and Rudi joined them, Jean saying, "We meet again."

"How lucky," Eustace said sourly. "I was afraid we'd lost you."

"And look who I found," Jean said, with a gesture at Rudi, whose fierce smile seemed to indicate that he really didn't mind at all if no one spoke a language he could understand.

"I see him," Eustace said. "And you brought him along."

Jean's smile turned rueful: "He more or less insisted."

"You can talk all you want," Rudi said, in German, smiling like a swordsman in all directions, "but I'm here."

Muttering in Italian, observing his countrymen and listening to all these other people, Vito said, "I've never felt so alone in all my life."

"Look," Lida said pointing toward Angelo and Rosa. "They're finishing."

"Good," said Eustace. "Time for us to take over."

✦

Angelo put a block in the half-full back of the truck, then trotted down the steps to Rosa, struggling upward with a block in her arms. "This," she said, "is the last of them."

"Good." Angelo took the block from her, carried it up to the truck, and was about to put it in when Rudi reached from inside the truck and took the block, saying, "Thanks. You're a sweetheart."

Angelo was so astounded he let Rudi take the block, then stared at Jean and Vito, also in the back of the truck.

"Au revoir," said Jean.

"Go back to Italy, you bad people," Vito said, and shook his bony old fist at them.

"Angelo!" cried Rosa. "Stop them!"

But it was too late. Eustace, in the cab of the truck with Lida, pressed the accelerator and the truck drove away, bouncing on the pavement, turning out of sight on the Rue de Harlay and driving on around the Palais de Justice.

Rosa actually ran after the truck for half a block, yelling and shouting, but the effort was so patently useless that she quickly gave it up and turned back to yell at Angelo instead: "They're getting away!" she screamed. "They're going off with *our money* and you're just standing there!"

Angelo, expressionless, stood on the narrow sidewalk, arms folded, and let Rosa rave on. She yelled, she screamed, she tore her hair, she beat her breast, she kicked parked cars, and at last she wound down and merely stood there panting, staring at Angelo, who continued to watch her as though she were a television set. "Well?" she finally gasped. "Well? What have you to say for yourself?"

"You," Angelo told her, "are a female impersonator." And he turned and walked away.

26

In the parking garage where first the gang had assembled, in the lowest parking level deep deep beneath the city, the twice-stolen truck rumbled at last to a stop. Rudi and Vito and Jean, all very cheerful, hopped down from the back. "We'll unload and make the split right here," Jean said, and turned to see the truck in motion again. "Wait!" he yelled.

In the truck cab, Lida looked at Eustace in some astonishment. "Eustace? Our friends aren't with us."

"Dear, dear," Eustace said.

"Stop!" yelled Jean and Rudi and Vito, in three languages, but the truck didn't stop. They ran after it, and the truck made a great sweeping U-turn in the nearly empty concrete space, and roared away again up the ramp it had just come down. The three men, knowing it was hopeless, stopped running at the base of the ramp and looked upward, hearing the truck engine quickly fade into silence.

"Bastard!" Vito yelled, shaking his fist at emptiness. "You took me out of retirement for *this?*"

Quietly, to the air, Rudi said, "I never trusted him. Never."

In English, Jean told the other two, "We can't let him get away with this."

"We have to follow him," Vito told the other two, "and murder him seven different ways, and get our money back."

"We have to get even somehow," Rudi told the other two.

Switching to French, Jean said, "We three will have to work together. We are all of us competent criminals in our own right, after all."

Emphatically, Rudi said, "Now we'll have to work together."

"We'll have to make plans together," Vito said.

Silence. The three men looked at one another expectantly. Gradually their confidence and determination faded away, and they finished by staring at one another in bewilderment.

Jean broke the unhappy silence. In English he said, "Neither of you speaks English?" And in French, "Not French either?"

Sadly shaking his head, Vito said, "Did neither of you study Italian in school?"

Rudi looked from face to face. "You have no German?"

Silence again, broken again by Jean: "How—"

Rudi: "When—"

Vito: "What—"

Another silence, and this time a kind of fatalism gradually overtook all three. They began to smile and shrug at one another, as though to say *what-the-hell*. With many rueful smiles and shrugs and hand gestures, they shook hands all around, and waved, and slowly backed away from one another.

"Au revoir," said Jean.

"Auf Wiedersehen," said Rudi.

"Ciao," said Vito.

27

With great concentration Eustace drove the stolen truck filled with stolen goods northward across Paris, while Lida continued to frown at him, in doubt and worry. At last she said, "Eustace?"

"Hmm?"

"Aren't we giving the others *any* money?"

Eustace smiled, and patted her knee. "More for us," he said.

"But that isn't proper!"

Regretfully, Eustace said, "I have to tell you something, Lida. The others all meant to cheat you."

Wide-eyed, she stared at him: "What?"

"Those were all hardened criminals, my dear," he told her. "Every last one of them. We had to have such people, of course, to do the job."

"Yes, of course," said the beautiful revolutionary.

"But the only way they'd agree to work," Eustace told her, "was if I promised we'd keep all the money for ourselves, and not give half back to Yerbadoro."

"What? The people's money!"

"I know, I know. The sweat of their brows."

"How could anyone be so low?"

"Well," Eustace said sadly, "when you associate with the criminal class, that's what you have to expect."

Frowning, Lida said, "Even that nice Sir Mortimer?"

"Him especially. 'Money is wasted on the poor,' he always says. 'That's why God gave it all to the rich.'"

Her expression becoming tender, Lida said, "Oh, Eustace. And you saved it for the peasants."

"They were never out of my mind," he said, giving her knee another little squeeze. "But here we are," he added, and braked the truck to a stop in front of an old stone building with a large garage-type entrance shut with two big green wooden doors.

Lida frowned out at the building. "What is this?"

"A special place," Eustace told her, taking the keys from the ignition. "A hideout nobody knows about." And he stepped out of the truck.

Lida didn't move. She looked out, seeing that they had come to a deserted steep narrow street in Montmartre, with no pedestrians and no traffic. Eustace came around to open her door for her, but she still didn't move. Frowning now at Eustace, she said, "But why do we have to hide? Why don't we go to the police?"

In a hurry to get himself and the truck under cover, Eustace impatiently said, "Because, my dear, we're hiding *from* the police."

"But why?"

Accepting the fact that he would have to give the girl an explanation, Eustace spoke with controlled haste: "Because," he said, "if we're caught with this part of the castle, the police will give it back to your President Lynch."

"But why?"

"Technically," Eustace reminded her, "it belongs to him. Now, come along, dear."

Still dubious, Lida at last stepped down out of the truck and walked with Eustace to the green garage doors, saying, "But shouldn't we get out of Paris, then?"

"Tomorrow," Eustace told her. "Our former friends are all over the city right now, so we should go to ground. We'll be perfectly safe here, I arranged this place myself. Nobody else knows about it." And Eustace pulled open the big green doors to show Herman standing there, a savage smile on his face. "So, Eustace," Herman said, "we meet again."

"Ack!" said Eustace, recoiling, throwing his hands up defensively. The truck keys, still in his right hand, leaped out of his grip and sailed up into the air, winking in the sunlight. Herman and Eustace both gaped at the keys rising through the air, but it was Lida who launched herself upward like a collie catching a rubber ball, snatched the keys at the apogee of their climb, and landed running.

For a second longer, both men merely stared, as Lida raced rapidly but gracefully away; then Herman brushed Eustace out of his way and went loping off after the girl like a wolf after a deer. "Wait!" cried Eustace, and joined the chase.

Lida made a turn at the corner, ran uphill, ran downhill, made another turn, and all at once she was in Montmartre Cemetery, a hilly ancient necropolis so crowded it gives the impression its citizens are buried standing up. Rushing in among the stones and mausoleums, Lida quickly was lost to sight.

Herman, still wolflike, entered the cemetery and quartered this way and that, as though trying to recapture a lost scent. Eustace, winded, barely entered the cemetery before

181

coming to a stop and leaning against a handy statue of a saint inexplicably holding a sword and a pineapple. When he'd caught his breath, Eustace shouted, "Lida! Look out for him, he's after you!"

No response. Amid the tall stones, statues, narrow outhouse-like mausoleums, Eustace caught occasional glimpses of Herman, inexorably moving, but of Lida he could see nothing. "Lida!" he shouted. "Head back this way, we'll fight him off together! Come around this way! Throw me the keys!"

Again there was no response from Lida, but now Herman too began to call out, in a hoarse but penetrating voice: "Lida!" he shouted, "listen to me! I came back to help you! Eustace meant to rob you!"

"He's a liar!" Eustace yelled. "Who could believe him? He's already betrayed us once!"

"That was to protect the money for you and Yerbadoro!" yelled the lying Herman. "I knew what they planned to do, all of them!"

"Lida!" cried Eustace. "We've been together from the beginning! You know you can believe me!"

"I am an officer and a gentleman!" roared Herman. "You can rely on me totally!"

"You've been *safe* with me, Lida!"

"Don't let Eustace catch you, Lida! He's desperate!"

A flash of color; both men saw it at once, and it was Lida, climbing over the low wall, picturesque with bird droppings. "Lida!" both men yelled, and both ran forward, and Lida was off again, racing like a rabbit on the cobblestone street, back in the direction she'd come from.

The truck was still parked at the now-open green door. Lida came around the corner below it, raced to the truck, and Herman appeared behind her, running hard; then Eustace, panting hard and weaving from side to side.

Lida jumped into the truck, fumbling with the keys, but there wasn't time to start the engine; Herman's image filled the rear view mirror. Frantic, Lida released the brake and clutch, and the truck rolled backward, rapidly gaining speed on the steep street.

Herman leaped toward the truck as it approached, but then had to leap again, out of its way, as it juggernauted by, Lida trying to steer backward and one-handed while straining her terrified head out the window. Eustace, staggering uphill, looked up to see the truck descending on him like a fly swatter on a fly; with a shriek, Eustace flung himself to the side and plastered himself against a wall as the truck thundered past.

When Eustace could next focus, it was to see the truck whipping away backward around a corner, while in the other direction Herman was hurriedly inserting himself into a small black Simca. Shaky but determined, Eustace unpeeled himself from the wall, ran across the street, and clambered into the passenger seat of the Simca just as Herman was starting its engine.

Herman glared, without friendliness. "Get out of here," he said. "*I* stole it, it's mine."

"I'm going with you," Eustace said. "Period."

There was really no time for Herman to argue the point. "Tchah," Herman said, in lieu of discussion, and spun the wheel. The Simca made a teetering U-turn and hurried after the truck.

Which had plummeted around another corner and was now backing rapidly *upward*, up another narrow street, which came to an abrupt end in midair, with a railing and a flight of stone steps downward. Lida, gaping backward, saw this sudden terminus of street, gave a despairing cry, and huddled down into the seat, eyes squeezed shut, hands over face.

The upgrade slowed the truck, slowed it, and at the very edge of the precipice the truck bunked gently against the iron railing, stopped, paused a millisecond, and began to roll forward.

On the next street, Eustace was pointing, saying, "She turned that way."

"I know," Herman said, and savagely spun the wheel, and the Simca roared around the corner to find the truck now racing forward, zooming down the street, knifing straight down at the Simca. "Mein Gott!" cried Herman, steering a thousand ways at once, while in the truck cab Lida could be seen struggling to insert the key in the ignition, paying no attention to steering or speed or anything else.

Herman got most of the Simca out of the way; most, but not all. The truck, *en passant*, nicked the Simca's left rear fender, clipping it just enough at exactly the moment when Herman had decided to turn sharply leftward, that as the truck roared on, its engine at last coughing into life, the Simca very slowly, very gracefully, almost casually, fell over onto its right side.

28

Pedestrians passing the ground floor offices of the Paris-based *International Herald Tribune* can look through the plate glass window imprinted in gold with the paper's name and see within a traditional newspaper office, with many desks and few workers and much buzzing purposeful activity. All this activity, however, came to an abrupt stop when without warning a truck came crashing and smashing through that plate glass window, trampled a couple of empty desks, and jolted to a stop half-in and half-out of the office.

The newspeople stared. A pin was heard to drop.

The truck door opened, and a shaky but triumphant Lida stepped out onto the running board. Gathering her strength, she raised an arm in a clenched-fist salute and gave voice: "Long live Yerbadoro!"

29

Fortunately, a photographer in the *Tribune*'s offices that day had been quickwitted enough to snap a picture of Lida in that moment of victory, creating an unforgettable and prize-winning image of Girl Revolutionary Rampant, a somewhat stylized drawing of which, superimposed with the word YERBADORO above and the words CORREO AEREO–1000 PESERINAS below, appeared on the stamp on the envelope containing the letter which, ten months later, a smiling Eustace read in the back seat of his limousine, traveling along Boulevard St. Germain on Paris's Left Bank. The letter read:

Dear Eustace,

Well, now that Manuel and I are back from our honeymoon, I am content to be merely a housewife from now on. Manuel has completely gotten over his distress and unhappiness, caused by that long dreadful wait in the hotel room, alone and friendless, never knowing what was going on, and he has now happily settled down to his Congressional duties.

I'm so glad, Eustace, that our political influence
helped to free you and your friends from prison,
and I hope you have made wise investments with the
reward money our new government gave you. You
know, in spite of everything, I still am fond of every
one of you.

Yours, for a progressive Yerbadoro,

Lida

"Ah, Lida," Eustace murmured, with another smile, and
he tucked the letter back into its envelope, paused for a
moment to study the dear girl's face on the stamp, then
pocketed the envelope as the limousine came to a stop at
the canopied entrance of a very elegant, very expensive, très
chic restaurant, its name emblazoned on the canopy: *Le
Yerbadoro*. Eustace waited, and his chauffeur—Bruddy, in
fact—came around to open the door for him. Eustace
emerged, smiled genially at the world around himself, and
said, "I think—ten tonight, Bruddy."

Nothing would ever make Bruddy actually deferential,
but his manner was at least calm and obliging as he said,
"Right," did not quite touch his uniform cap, and drove
the limousine away.

Eustace approached the restaurant's entrance, where
Jean, resplendent in his doorman's uniform, stood holding
open the door. "Afternoon, Jean," said Eustace.

"Afternoon, Eustace. Lovely day."

"Lovely."

Eustace entered the restaurant and smiled upon the
cashier, who happened to be Maria Lynch, one time First
Lady of Yerbadoro, wife of the former El Presidente. Discreet enquiries and delicate negotiations had been necessary
before Escobar and Maria Lynch had been persuaded to

join Eustace and the others, but it was only sensible for the forces to combine, and in the end sensibility won the day. The Lynches' hidden hoard had been lost to them forever, but there was still the rest of the castle, containing much of value. The Lynches held title, Eustace and company held the castle, and a meeting of minds was seen to be possible.

"Lovely day," Eustace told Maria, who was at the moment frowning in disapproval at a stack of checks from lunch. She looked up, transferring her frown to Eustace: "Going to rain tomorrow," she said.

"Ah, well, perhaps," said Eustace, and passed on into the restaurant proper, a plush hushed room with a distinct South American flavor. The last of the luncheon diners were gone, the first of the dinner diners had not as yet arrived, and to one side headwaiter Herman was speaking very severely to his staff of waiters: Rudi, Angelo, Vito and Otto. "Last night," Herman was saying, marching stiffly back and forth before his troops, "there were three complaints about delays in service. Tonight we shall do better. You *will* do better, and you *will* smile."

Eustace moved on, just glancing in at the bar, where Andrew and Sir Mortimer were already at work, preparing for the evening's custom. Continuing, Eustace passed the blackly gleaming grand piano, where Charles in a tuxedo tickled the ivories while chatting with Renee, the cigarette girl. Beyond, Eustace just opened the kitchen door and glanced in, seeing Rosa, in chef's cap and apron, yelling at her Portuguese staff in every language she knew and some she didn't. Eustace closed the door again and continued to the very rear of the restaurant, where the sommelier, Escobar Diaz McMahon Grande Pajaro Lynch, ex-El Presidente of Yerbadoro, stood frowning at a bottle of wine. Eustace said, "Everything all right?"

"Perhaps not," said Escobar. "I think this St. Emilion has started to turn."

"Then don't give it to any Frenchmen," Eustace said. "Scandinavians, English and Americans only."

Escobar was too professional to be insulted. "Of course," he said, and put the bottle down.

Smiling, Eustace turned to survey his domain. "You know," he said, "I would never have guessed it, but there is something pleasant about being an honest man."